Clutch
the Trucking Cat

Joie and Amanda Flickinger

PublishAmerica
Baltimore

ISBN: 1-4241-9535-7
PUBLISHED BY PUBLISHAMERICA, LLLP
www.publishamerica.com
Baltimore

Printed in the United States of America

* * *

We'd love to dedicate this to our pen pal students, and to Jean Herring, my fith grade teacher, who taught me to appreciate the written word, as well as Mr. Walker who taught me how to go after my dreams no matter how big or small. For my neice Mindy, who has been with us from day one of this, we can't thank you enough. Uncle Buzz, where ever you are we still love you! Aunt Mae, you're even more cool in life, and special then our stories. Also Boys, we love you! There wouldn't be stories without you!

* * *

Not so long ago, in a small farming town in Indiana, Tabby, the pretty farm cat gave birth to six beautiful kittens. She had four girls and two boys. Tabby was a great mother and the best mouser on the Dobsin farm. She took the very best care of her kittens. She took always the time to listen to them and lightly scolded them when they misbehaved.

The kittens spent their days playing and chasing their tails, then taking long naps in the warm sunlight. All of the kittens had dreams of drinking milk, eating cheese, and catching mice—that is, all but one. He had dreams of cups full of coffee, bowls full of chili, and driving a truck. His brother and sisters would laugh and tease him when he talked about his dreams. They would tell him, "Trucks are for humans. No matter how much you want to drive a big truck, you will always be a cat."

His mother would always patiently listen when the kittens talked about their dreams. When her son spoke of wanting to drive a truck she would look at him strangely, smile, and say, "It's okay to dream about things others do not."

One day, when Mr. Dobsin's nephew came to visit in a freightliner, Tabby's youngest kitten tried hard to climb up the steps into the truck. Pete Dobsin saw the kitten trying to get into his truck and found himself laughing.

His uncle jokingly said, "Pete, Son, you oughta take him with ya'. Maybe you can teach him to drive." They laughed harder.

Pete said, "I would, but he's too small. He still needs his momma."

Tabby was very proud of all of her kittens. It made her angry when the humans made fun of them.

The next afternoon, when the kittens lay down in the sun to take a nap, Tabby asked her son to talk to her a bit. She carefully told him, "Son, I love you very much. I want you to have good dreams, but you must face reality. One day you will grow up to be a fine, proud tomcat. You should try to learn how to do cat things such as chase butterflies and catch mice. Farmers always need good mousers. They reward with fresh cream. Now take a nap like a good kitten."

* * *

About two weeks later Mrs. Dobsin drove the pick-up truck into town for groceries. When she came home Mr. Dobsin helped her to carry supplies into the house. She realized she left the truck door open. When she went out to close it she saw a kitten standing on the steering wheel. He was also batting at the gearshift. She called her husband over her shoulder, "Bill, that little guy is trying to drive!"

Her husband then told her all about their nephew's last visit.

Tabby saw the humans laughing at her kitten's actions and was deeply offended. The word quickly spread all over the farm. Soon, even the rabbits were laughing. She did not know what to do.

It upset her greatly to have anyone make fun of her kitten, especially since he had done nothing wrong. She decided to go to the wisest animal on the farm.

Boots was the head cow and was accepted as the wisest animal on the farm. After listening to Tabby, she turned to the kitten and kindly suggested, "Try to cluck like a chicken."

He tried, but failed to do so. After a while he hung his head low and mewed, "I can't."

Then she said, "Try to squeal like a pig."

He could not do that either.

Next she asked, "Can you quack like a duck?"

After several tries, he had to admit that he couldn't.

Finally, she told him, "Moo like a cow."

With many strange sounds, he had to admit he could do none of these things.

She looked at him and gently stated, "I am a cow, so I can not meow like a cat. I am what I am. You, Little One, are what you are. Run along like a good little kitten. I will see about extra cream tonight."

He went to where his brother and sisters were taking their naps. Instead of joining them, he curled up into a ball all alone and cried himself to sleep.

* * *

That night he was awakened by the Great Tomcat of the Woods. The big cat sternly demanded of him, "I saw you crying today. Why?"

The tiny kitten sighed. "I often have dreams of driving a big truck, but I can't because I'm just a cat."

The Great Tom Cat proudly said, "I am what I want to be. No cat should be anything less than what he can be. I don't moo, cluck, squeal, or heaven forbid quack. I am what I choose to be. I am what I've always dreamed of being. You should never settle for anything less. It's okay to dream of being different."

In the morning he was awakened by a vehicle with a large rolling motor. Pete Dobsin had come to his uncle's farm for another visit. As the truck came to a halt, Bill Dobsin came out of the milk barn to greet his nephew. "Say Pete, ya' got another one, do ya'?"

"Yeah," replied Pete proudly. "I just picked her up in Indy. As of now she has seventy-five on her."

Uncle Bill whistled at the shiny red truck. "She's a real beauty. I just got done milking. Let's you and me go get some of your aunt's good breakfast cooking. Pete, don't forget to close the door on your rig. That kitten might just try to drive off with your truck!"

* * *

During breakfast Aunt Mae told the story about the kitten trying to drive the pick-up.

Pete laughed so hard he almost choked on his coffee.

She teased, "Son, I hope you closed the door of your truck. You don't want that little furball taking your job from you."

They all laughed.

Pete was on his fourth cup of coffee when they heard an air horn blow.

Bill looked startled. "It can't be the milk truck. He came yesterday. Someone's messing with your truck!"

About that time the airhorn blew again. They all ran outside to see what was going on.

As they approached the truck the city horn blew. Pete had left the window open. As he yanked open the door, he was surprised to see a kitten sitting on the steering wheel. Somehow the kitten had climbed the steps, jumped up onto the hood, climbed across the mirror bracket, and leaped through the window.

Uncle Bill yelled at the kitten. "You get out of there!"

Pete laughed and said, "Uncle Bill, don't yell at him. He's the one who tried to get into the truck the last time I was here. If you don't mind, I'd like to keep him. Who knows, maybe we can drive team."

They all laughed.

"Seriously, I think he'll be good company for me," Pete said.

Tabby watched in horror as the Dobsins caught her son in Pete's truck. Her fears quickly disappeared when she realized they were not angry with him. She was more than proud of her son as she listened to what the humans had to say.

Aunt Mae smiled softly. "Pete, you should ask his momma. After all, he is her baby."

Pete gently picked up the kitten and knelt down next to Tabby. "Tabby, it sure gets lonely out there, and I would be very, very honored if you would allow your son to travel with me. I promise to take excellent care of him. I also promise we'll come back and visit often."

Tabby rubbed noses with her son and purred as Pete scratched her ears. All the animals were proud of the kitten, even Scrappy the dog.

After a fine lunch, and the kitten having a chance to spend some time with his friends, Aunt Mae informed Pete that there were a few things that he and his young friend would be needing. She took him into town with her, picked him up a few supplies, and explained some secrets that only a good cat owner would know. "Let's see Pete, food dish, water dish—kittens need lots of water, litter pan and litter, plenty of toys—watch that catnip, kitten chow. You do not want to give him people food. He'll probably cry a lot at first. You will want to pick him up some just to let him know he's okay, but not all the time. He'll need rules. You don't want to let him get away with everything. Just treat him like he's your child."

After they returned to the farm, Pete put his supplies into his truck, gathered up his kitten, and everyone said their goodbyes. He turned to his kitten and said, "Come on little fellow. It's time to start our adventures."

As Pete opened the door of his truck, Uncle Bill asked, "Whatcha gonna call him?"

Pete set his kitten down on the floorboard and asked, "Well, what do you want me to call you?"

The kitten looked up at him and placed both paws on the clutch pad and meowed.

Pete looked at the kitten and smiled. "You got it. I'll call you Clutch."

Aunt Mae asked, "What kind of name is 'Clutch' for a cat?"

Uncle Bill put his arm around his wife and replied, "Mae, it's the perfect name. He's not just a cat. He's a trucking cat."

After another round of hugs and goodbyes Pete and Clutch started down the lane.

They had only driven a couple of minutes when Pete turned down another lane. Pete turned to Clutch and gently informed him, "This is where we live Clutch. Since my folks passed, Uncle Bill and Aunt Mae watch over it for me. He tends to my beef cows and cuts the hay for his cows and mine. Aunt Mae and Uncle Bill are the only family I have since my parents passed. Come in and I'll show you around. We'll be here for two days and then we'll leave out. I've got some chores to do."

Before they left out, Pete took a baby quilt out of a trunk and said to Clutch, "My mother made this for me before I was born. I'm giving this to you for your bed. Be careful with it. She put a lot of love into it." Then they left out.

They had driven about two hours when they arrived in Gary, Indiana where Pete fueled his truck and reefer unit. "Okay Partner, you've got guard duty." Pete went inside, paid for his fuel, coffee, and a large cup of chili to go.

When Pete returned to his truck he placed both the coffee and the chili into cup holders and rewarded his faithful kitten with a few soft treats.

Putting his truck into gear he said, "It's three days to Salt Lake City, and we're burning day light." As they passed through Ottawa, Illinois Pete downed his coffee and told Clutch, "I'll eat my chili later. It usually tastes better cold."

Several hours later, Pete pulled into his favorite truck stop in

Lincoln, Nebraska. Pete looked at Clutch, who was chasing his tail, and said, "Partner, if you're going to be out here with me, you need to start learning the ropes. We'll shut down here for ten hours and then we'll push on to Laramie, Wyoming."

Realizing he was tired, Pete decided he would take his full ten hours. He figured he could eat his chili for breakfast. He made sure Clutch had plenty of food and water and then curled up in the bunk to catch some sleep.

After Pete woke up and dressed, he realized things were way too quiet for having a kitten in the truck. When he opened the curtain, he saw a large mess on the floor. Clutch had knocked the cup of chili out of the cup holder and half of his coffee was gone. There were paw prints on the seat, steering wheel, and dash. There was also a small ball of fur curled on his seat with a red-orange smear on his face. Pete groaned at the mess. "There's something Aunt Mae forgot to tell me. It looks like I'm going to need lots of cleaning supplies."

Pete tried to be mad, but all he could do was shake his head and smile. "What is Aunt Mae going to say? And what am I going to eat now?" Pete brought out the paper towels and burst out laughing, which roused the innocently sleeping kitten.

He looked at Pete as if to say, "You woke me up!" The kitten yawned, stretched, and headed straight towards the litter pan to really raise a stink.

Pete quickly wound down the window and told Clutch over his shoulder, "Make sure you bury that!" Pete quickly rolled the window back up and stepped out into open air.

* * *

After a trip to the market Pete hung his new air freshener, put his new cleaning supplies away, and sat down to eat his burgers.

After buckling in to drive, he smiled at Clutch and sighed, "Little Buddy, I wish you came with an instruction booklet. Uncle Bill said you were mischievous, but I have a feeling that's an understatement."

The kitten just cocked his head to one side as if he understood everything. He then jumped up onto Pete's lap and curled into a ball to fall asleep purring.

Pete whispered with a smile, "We're gonna be all right, aren't we?"

The next day they stopped at a truck stop in Laramie, Wyoming. Pete told Clutch, "The food here isn't much but the coffee is great. You wait here and I'll be right back."

While he was inside, he met up with a driver from his company. "Hey Brenda," he said. "Wait until you see what's in my truck."

"Pete, this better not be a pick up line!" They both laughed and walked out to the truck where Clutch was dutifully sitting on the driver's seat.

Pete smiled and said, "Brenda, this is my partner, Clutch. He might just drive team with me when he grows up."

She looked at this cream-colored kitten with his black-tipped ears, black tail, and blue eyes. "Hey Clutch, it's good to meet you. My name is Brenda. My friends call me Daddy's Girl. Dad is a trucker, so like father like daughter. I see you fancy yourself a 'trucking cat.' Well you ain't much of a cat without a collar." Brenda gave Pete a stern look. "Don't you go just yet. I'll be right back."

15

She walked over to her truck. She returned a few minutes later and put a cheap watch around Clutch's neck. "Now you'll always know what time it is, and you'll never be late." She turned to Pete and proclaimed, "Now he's a trucking cat."

Clutch just purred.

* * *

After Pete and Brenda parted ways, she called to Pete on CB channel 19. "Hey Lone Wolf, take care of Clutch. It will be good for you not to be alone."

Pete teased, "Thanks Daddy's Girl. You know, it would be even less lonely if you were part of the pack."

She laughed and teased, "I might just consider it. Is that a proposal? Ask me sweetly and I might just think about it. But be careful what you say. You might end up with a collar on you too. Anyway, take good care of him. He's real special. Besides, cats are good luck."

They both laughed again and went their separate ways.

Pete turned to Clutch who was sitting in the jump seat, "Partner, let's get to Salt Lake before we really get into trouble."

Clutch growled trying to get the thing off his neck.

Pete laughed. "Well, let's go. We're burning daylight. I want to cross the Twin Sisters before the animals start to roam the pass into Salt Lake." He shifted gears and they left out. "We'll be there in about 7 hours."

They drove for what seemed like forever to Clutch. He jumped up onto the dash and stretched out for a contented catnap.

As Pete pulled off into a brake check area Clutch roused from his slumber, giving a long stretch. Pete scratched his ears and softly said, "See all those lights? As far as the eye can see, that's Salt Lake City. Really something to see, right boy?"

Clutch looked around at the lights in the distance. They reminded him of the fireflies back at home on the farm.

As they drove on into the city Clutch became quite aware of all the traffic speeding by.

Pete looked at his furry friend, sensing his worries. "Don't worry about them. They're in a hurry to go nowhere fast. We'll just keep it safe and legal. There we go. A right off this exit, then the first left, and we're here."

As Pete pulled onto the warehouse lot, the security guard walked up to Pete's parked truck and said, "Early again, as usual. You know where to park. They'll wake ya' in the morning."

Clutch growled at the stranger standing on the running boards. Pete looked at the guard and said, "Tom, this is Clutch. He's my guard cat."

Tom laughed at Clutch and replied, "He doesn't look like more than a ball of spit and fur, but I better watch out. He looks like he could be mighty mean."

They laughed.

"I have a fresh pot of coffee going," Tom told Pete. "Sorry Clutch, no cream."

Pete smiled and announced, "That's okay, he drank mine black."

Tom said, "I hope you didn't give him coffee."

Pete replied, "Nope. He just helped himself. My chili, too." They continued to laugh. "I'll be in for coffee when they put me into a door, but for now I want to check out the backs of my eyelids. Good night, Tom."

* * *

At 7:30 a.m. Mindy Parsons knocked on Pete's door to wake him. "Put 'er in door 6. We need that candy now, Pete. Call your boss while we reload you for Sacramento. Get some coffee in the meantime. By the way, what's that furry thing on your dash?"

Pete cheerfully replied, "And a good morning to you too Mindy. This is Clutch. He's my new partner."

Mindy just shook her head smiling. "Looks like you got your work cut out for ya'. I guess the Lone Wolf ain't so lone anymore. Good morning Clutch. Keep him straight, ya' here?"

Clutch purred.

Mindy looked at Pete and said, "Tom says he's got a fresh pot again. I'll see if I can find something better for your partner." Mindy brought Clutch a small bowl of milk. "I'll come get you when you're loaded."

Pete got his coffee and called dispatch.

* * *

Four hours later, they were reloaded and headed west. Pete looked at his partner as they crossed the salt flats leading into Nevada. "What do you think Partner? Pretty big litter box out there, right? We'll stop for the night at Reno. We don't deliver until tomorrow afternoon so there's plenty of time to get there and rest up again."

As they were pulling into Winnemucca, Nevada, Clutch looked at Pete and placed his right paw on his food dish. Pete smiled at him and said, "You're reading my mind, Partner. We'll pull into the truck stop and get some grub."

After Pete parked, he faithfully filled Clutch's food and water dishes and went inside to get some fried chicken and potato wedges for himself.

When he returned to his truck he saw his kitten enjoying a cool drink of water. Pete smiled. "You know Partner, that's not a bad idea." He went into the bunk to get himself a cold bottle of soda from the cooler. He took a long pull on his cola and returned up front. Clutch had taken one of his potato wedges and was going to town.

"Hey! Eat your own food! Do you want Aunt Mae to skin us both? What's wrong with your food?" He laughed. As Pete grabbed a drumstick Clutch tried to take it from him. "Not this time, Bud. I'm eating this." Clutch just looked at him. "If you mind your manners, I might leave a little meat on the bone for you."

Clutch purred.

Pete was just finishing his snack when his cell phone rang. It was Aunt Mae.

"Well how are my two boys doing?" she asked.

"We're fine," he blushed.

"Are you treating him good? How's he taking to the truck? Is he box training? Is he behaving good? Another thing—"

Pete interrupted. "Really Aunt Mae, we're both doing great. We're not having any problems," Pete lied. "You don't have to worry ma'am. Everything is fine. Don't forget that we came from good stock."

Clutch was batting at the antenna and meowing loudly.

"I think he misses you Aunt Mae. Want to talk to him?"

"Put him on," she replied. "Looky here fellow. Pete's a hard workin' man. Don't you go givin' him any fits. You're a big cat now. I'm counting on you to take good care of Pete. He's the only family we got."

Clutch answered, "Meow!"

Aunt Mae talked to Pete again. "I don't know what you boys are up to, but I smell something and you ain't scraping the barnyard." Aunt Mae was silent for a moment. She finally spoke just above a whisper, "I worry about you when you're gone Peter. You boys just be safe." She wiped away a tear.

"I love you too Aunt Mae."

The conversation ended.

Pete wiped away the wetness of his eyes. "It's getting warm in here. Let's kick on the air conditioner."

Clutch climbed up onto Pete's shoulder and rubbed his head on Pete's cheek, purring.

Pete hugged his kitten and sighed. "Come on Partner. We're burning day light." He wiped the moisture from his face again, put his truck into gear, and they were back on their way.

Several hours later, they pulled into the truck stop in Reno. Pete looked at Clutch and said, "This place doesn't look like much, but there's plenty of parking and the food is great. Why, I think they even hired real cooks." Once again Pete checked Clutch's dishes and said, "You've got guard duty again. I'm going to get me a shower. Don't let anyone take off with our truck.

After Pete ate and returned to the truck he said, "I brought you something Partner." Pete pulled out two shrimp that were wrapped in a napkin. "Don't get too used to this. That's for guard duty. Come on. Let's catch some Z's." Clutch quickly wolfed down the shrimp and went to his cat bed.

A few hours later Pete was awakened by a vibration. Clutch was curled up in a ball next to his head purring in his sleep. "Well so much for the cat bed." Pete just pulled his sheet up a little more to tuck in his kitten and drifted back to sleep.

* * *

Pete was awake by 7 o'clock a.m. and faithfully filled Clutch's dishes and cleaned the litter pan.

Clutch sat on the passenger seat inspecting Pete's work and promptly let go of some gas.

Pete very quickly rolled down the window. "I wish you could give me some kind of warning when you're going to do that. I think I better put spray air freshener on the shopping list. That hanging air freshener just doesn't cut it."

Clutch just smiled at him.

"Let's get out of here."

After about 45 minutes they pulled into a California weigh station in Truckee.

When Pete came to a stop on the scale, the scale master commanded through the speaker, "Wendover, take your truck around the building and line up behind Inspection Bay 3."

Pete did as he was instructed.

Thirty minutes later a female inspector said to him, "Okay, Wendover. You've earned your sticker. Lookin' good."

Pete smiled and teased, "You too, Officer."

She grinned. "Be careful. You could get into trouble for that."

Pete inquired, "With the law?"

She answered, "No. With my husband." Looking at Clutch she asked, "Are you going to teach him how to drive?"

Pete replied, "I might as well. He already knows how to blow the air horn."

They both laughed. She then scolded Pete, "Get out of here. You've got a truck payment to make!"

Once again they were on the go.

J ust a few hours later Pete and Clutch reached their final destination.

As they pulled into the guard shack they were informed that they were two hours early. After the guard called the receiving office he told Pete the product was very much needed. He should put it in door 105. Pete carried his bills to the receiving window. The receiver informed him that he would be unloaded immediately. The product was needed to fill orders. "Don't even bother going back to your truck. I'm putting three forklift drivers on it. You'll be done in twenty minutes."

Pete went to the drivers' lounge to call his boss.

"Hey, Rob," Pete said. "By the time we finish this call, I'll be empty."

"Good job! That load was listed as hot freight. You'll get a $200 bonus on that one. The bad news is you don't pick up until tomorrow in Fresno. Can you have that one in South Jersey in, say, six days?"

Pete replied, "By early evening, yes. You know me Rob, only by the rules."

His boss replied that he didn't want it any other way. "Besides, your delivery in Jersey is an open window until midnight."

"It sounds good to me," Pete replied. "What will I be hauling?"

Rob answered, "Twenty-five thousand pounds of high dollar pet supplies. We booked three for tomorrow. There's a good bonus for on-time delivery."

Pete laughed. "Maybe I can get a few things for my cat. Just kidding. I wouldn't ask."

Rob laughed. "By the way, how is that little kitten taking to the road?"

Pete replied, "He's doing great. He was born for it."

As Pete was headed back to his truck a young man handed Pete his bills. "You have a great day."

"You're gonna love this next load—and entire load of kitty toys," Pete told Clutch as he was climbing back into the truck.

Clutch just looked at Pete.

"Let's head down to Ripon and get a parking spot while we still can."

Clutch meowed.

Pete turned his truck south on Route 99.

An hour later they exited at the Ripon off ramp and pulled into one of the three truck stops. As Pete backed into a parking spot, a medium-sized man walked up to the shiny red freightliner.

As Pete shut off the engine, "I see you got a new one Lone Wolf."

Pete smiled. "Yes sir! She's on her maiden run. How have you been Mr. Kingman?"

The older gentleman, with long graying hair covered by a Stetson, smiled back and replied, "Doin' good, Son. You haven't seen my little girl out here have you? It's been a couple of months since she and I had coffee together. Oh well. They don't call me 'Too Long' for nothin'."

Pete smiled and answered, "I saw Brenda about five days ago at Laramie. She was headed east."

"Oh well," said Too Long. "Maybe I'll see her the next time I'm through the house. Let's go get a bite to eat. What the heck is that on your seat?"

"That's my new partner," said Pete. "His name is Clutch. Let's go inside and I'll tell you all about him." Pete closed and locked the door, and the two men went inside.

The elder of the two men smiled and stated, "It's not the fanciest place around but the food sure is good here."

While waiting for their waitress, Pete told the story of how Clutch tried to drive his truck.

After he finished Tom Kingman smiled and said, "It's not a bad idea to have a pet to keep you company, but maybe you oughta think about havin' a partner—drive team. If I remember right, you two were the top of the class."

Pete smiled. "Yeah, we tied on everything, except one test. She beat me by two points. Wouldn't it look kind of funny?"

The older man grew quiet. "Son, I'm not talking about—just at the mention of your name, she's a different person. And don't think I don't see the way you smile at the mention of hers. I don't want to see her turn out like me. She's my only child and I don't want her to have my regrets. I just think the pair of you would be a great team. So am I any good at playing matchmaker?"

"Yup." Pete nodded his head. "I guess every dad wants the best for their children. I don't know about that. If I were to settle down, I can't think of anybody finer. I don't think I would be much of a prize though."

Tom snorted. "If I didn't think you were the right stuff I sure wouldn't be stickin' my nose where it doesn't belong. Besides, I can't think of anyone better for you. Son, I've been out here for 35 years. Thirty-five years of missing birthdays, holidays, and even a couple of wedding anniversaries. For 35 years I've been a stranger to my family. My Phyllis stood by me for every day of it. Son, when this load is finished I'm turning in my keys. I might find something local to drive, but I want to get to know my family again. My daughter chose to follow in my footsteps, but sometimes these are shoes I don't want to wear anymore."

With that, the door opened in the café. A beautiful woman walked up to their table and gave Tom and hug from behind. Pete looked at her with surprise. He exclaimed, "Brenda, I thought you were headed east!"

She smiled and replied, "I was but Red Dog had an emergency back home. We swapped loads at York, Nebraska. I took his load to Tracy, California, and he took mine back to Indy. He just called me on the cell phone to thank me. He made it just in time for the birth of his first grandchild."

Too Long smiled at his daughter and she chided him, "I know what you're thinking. Don't go there."

Tom looked proudly at his daughter. "You can't blame a man for wanting."

Pete smiled silently.

Brenda growled at Pete. "Are you going to move over or am I going to have to just stand here?"

Pete, embarrassed, quickly moved over so Brenda could sit down.

The oldest of the three smiled and stated, "We were just talking about you."

She answered, "I bet you were."

Pete struggled with his words. "Well, we weren't saying anything bad."

She pointed a finger at her dad. "This old fart was probably trying to play matchmaker again."

Too Long caught his daughter's finger and laughed, "Like I said, you can't blame a man for wanting."

Brenda looked at Pete and softly asked, "So what do you think?"

Pete looked at her for a long moment and said with a red face, "I don't think I want to say anything."

Just then the waitress brought them menus.

After dinner the three of them talked over coffee and pie. Tom looked at Brenda and calmly said, "I wanted to keep it a surprise. Don't tell your momma, but this is my last run. Too Long has been gone too long. I want to get to know your mother again. She's a wonderful woman and deserves a full-time husband. I've decided that it's time for me to go home."

Brenda put her hands over her father's hands. With a tearful smile she said, "I love you, Daddy."

To change the subject, she turned to Pete and said, "I have something to show you in my truck."

Pete teased, "Tom you better come along and make sure she's on the up and up."

Brenda slapped Pete on the knee then growled, "Don't go there, Lone Wolf."

The two men laughed.

The three of them walked out to Brenda's truck. She unlocked her door and pulled out a beautiful calico kitten. Brenda softly said, "I found her at a rest area in Nebraska. The attendant told me somebody just dropped her off the day before. I couldn't just let her starve! Isn't she beautiful? Her name is Calli."

Pete cleared his throat and asked, "So what are you loading?"

She answered, "Picking up pet supplies in Fresno tomorrow. The load is going back to Jersey."

Pete smiled and replied, "Me too."

Tom exclaimed, "Great! You two can run it together."

Brenda frowned. "Daddy," she warned.

Tom hugged and kissed his daughter on her cheek. "You two have a safe trip. I'm already going home. See you there, Girl. I'll be the one planting tomatoes, flowers, and whatever else your mother wants. See ya'!" Her father left them with a contented smile on his face.

The next day, around noon, Pete and Brenda turned their rigs south. About 2 hours later, they both backed into doors at the Whiskers and Paws warehouse. After they checked in at the shipping office, Pete looked at the young lady and inquired, "I thought there were three loads coming out."

The lady replied, "We'll load the third tonight. They run team and won't be here for a couple of hours."

Brenda smiled and asked, "Pet toys, huh? Have any free samples?"

"Sure," replied the young lady. "Do you have pets? Come inside and we'll fix you up. What do you have?"

"Kittens," answered Pete. "Mine's a male. Hers is female."

The lady smiled. "Why don't you bring them in? They are allowed. These are pet supplies after all."

Pete and Brenda dutifully retrieved their pets.

As they were returning to the warehouse Clutch tried to sniff at Brenda's kitten, but she ignored him.

Inside Monica asked them, "What are their names?"

Pete showed his kitten and replied, "This is Clutch."

Brenda smiled and said, "Her name is Calli."

The lady smiled and replied, "I'm sorry we don't have any treats. We specialize in toys. Well you both can wait in your trucks and I'll pick out some fun stuff for your babies."

Brenda and Pete looked at each other strangely.

The young lady stated, "I was referring to your kittens. Now put your radios on channel 15 and I'll call you."

A few hours later the call came across both radios, "Okay both Wendovers come and get your bills."

Both Pete and Brenda went into the shipping office to get their bills and sign for their loads.

The lady handed each of them a plastic shopping bag saying, "This one is for Mr. Clutch, and this one is for Miss Calli."

They both thanked her. "I believe there's something in there for both of them. There's even some catnip in there. Have a safe trip you two."

Pete and Brenda thanked her again. They returned to their trucks, climbed in, and closed their doors.

Before leaving, Brenda shyly asked Pete, "What channel do we use?"

Pete replied, "Let's go to 19 for now, and if you want some privacy we can go to 34."

Brenda nodded in agreement.

They got into their trucks and placed their radios on the perspective channels.

Brenda keyed her mike, "Who's leading?"

Pete replied, "I'll watch your tail, er, I'll bring up the back." They then headed south towards Bakersfield.

After about a half hour, Brenda called out on her radio, "Hey Lone Wolf, how do you want to run this one?"

Pete responded, "Let's run CA 58 to Barstow, hop on 15 north to I-40 east, then I-81 north. We'll work out the rest from there. It's about 150 miles farther than running through Denver, but its 3 hours quicker, and it sure saves on the fuel. Where do you suggest we let our cats out for a break?"

Brenda suggested, "How about Flagstaff?"

Pete agreed, "That will be about right. How much weight do you have?"

She answered, "I have 23,900 pounds. How about you?"

Pete replied, "I have 27,650."

Brenda teased, "Funny, you don't look an ounce over 200 to me."

Pete said, "HA, HA, HA, very funny." Pete changed the subject.

"Hey Daddy's Girl, did you look at the stuff they gave us? I never realized there was so much stuff for cats."

Brenda replied, "This is nothing. This is just some of the small stuff for cats. She gave Calli 10 different bows that clip onto her collar and a straw hat that has holes notched into it for her ears."

Pete said, "Yeah, Clutch got a red baseball cap and a 4-pack of bandana collars."

All the while the kittens examined the bags and looked at their drivers with disgust.

Brenda added, "They're gonna look so pretty."

Without thinking Pete said, "And so do you."

Clutch nipped Pete on the ankle.

Pete looked down at him.

Clutch was shaking his head as if he was telling him no.

Pete keyed up, "I don't think Clutch wants to look pretty."

Brenda answered, "Do you really think I look pretty? Lone Wolf, are you interested?"

Pete stammered, "Well, yes! I mean, well, um…" Pete cleared his throat and changed the subject. "Do you have plenty of cool drinks? It's going to be hot going across the desert."

Brenda laughed. "I think I just embarrassed you. Anyway, my cooler is fine. I just put in fresh ice this morning."

Pete was quiet for a moment then replied, "We're good too. Let's stop in Barstow for a short bit to stretch our legs and grab some coffee. Clutch just knocked mine over and started drinking it.

Brenda chuckled and said, "You two shouldn't drink so much coffee. And you need to behave better or I'm going to bring a leash out for the both of you."

Pete went silent again.

As they climbed out of their trucks and stretched, Brenda asked, "Do you want to get something for dinner?"

Pete took a long look at her, distracted by how beautiful she really was. "I missed that. You know, truck noises. Could you repeat that?"

Brenda stretched again and then softly asked, "What would you like to do for dinner?"

"Why don't we just grab something to hold us over? There's a really nice restaurant at Flagstaff beside the truck stop," offered Pete.

Brenda smiled. "Peter Dobsin, are you asking me out on a date?"

Pete looked at her strangely and then said, "Yes, I am Brenda."

She looked at him for a long while before accepting, a faint hint of pink touching her cheeks.

After they left both drivers went on standby. As they cleared the Arizona port of entry, Brenda keyed up and asked, "Shall I wear a dress to dinner?"

Pete answered shyly, "Whatever you want will be fine. I have to warn you, I don't exactly carry a suit with me."

Brenda replied, "Since it's our first date, let's deck out the best we can. I want to shower first though."

Pete replied, "I could use one myself. I think you'll find this Indiana farm boy is capable of scrubbing up."

* * *

After their showers, they rejoined each other by the front desk. Mr. Dobsin exclaimed, "Brenda you really do know how to scrub."

Pete was wearing navy blue dress pants, a short sleeve white, button-up shirt, and 2-tone blue clip-on tie that accented his blue eyes. His wavy brown hair was well kept, and his boots were well polished.

"I almost didn't recognize you Miss Kingman. You're absolutely beautiful."

Brenda blushed. She was wearing a knee length, simple but classy powder blue dress. Her long, reddish tan hair was gracefully pulled back into a lovely golden clasp. White casual shoes finished her carefully planned attire.

Pete and Brenda silently gazed at one another for a few moments before Pete's stomach growled loudly.

Pete smiled and softly requested, "Shall we go to dinner?"

Brenda laughed nervously. "I would be honored, Mr. Dobsin."

The two strolled arm in arm to their trucks where they deposited their grips and checked on their kittens.

When Brenda suggested perhaps the kittens should spend some time together, Pete agreed. Brenda asked, "Why don't you go get

Clutch while I get a can of crabmeat for them to share. After all, if we have fine dining, shouldn't they too?"

Pete again agreed and went to his truck to get Clutch. A few moments later he returned with Clutch and placed him in Brenda's truck.

"Clutch, I hope you will be a gentleman with the young lady," Pete told him.

Brenda told Calli, "Calli, I hope your conduct yourself as a young lady."

After closing the door, Pete and Brenda strolled across the parking lot passing shocked onlookers.

Brenda glanced at them and smiled, sliding her hand under Pete's as they then crossed the parking lot to go inside.

For the longest while, Clutch looked at Calli, but neither one would speak.

Calli simply ignored him.

Eventually the smell of crabmeat caught Clutch's nose. He walked over to the dish to smell and taste the food.

"That's my dish!" snarled Calli. "If you really want to try it you should at least ask first!"

"I'm sorry," sighed Clutch.

"I think the way to do that is to say 'please,' at least that's what I heard my human say," Calli snorted. "Besides, I should probably try this stuff first."

Clutch stepped away from the food dish and sat down. He meowed plaintively, "By all means, it is your food dish."

Calli jumped off the driver's seat, strolled past Clutch with her nose in the air, and strutted to the food dish. She sniffed at the crabmeat and turned her head to stare at Clutch. "You gotta try this stuff. It's great."

Clutch walked over and put his head into the dish. He looked at Calli before he tasted the food. With a mouth full of crabmeat Clutch exclaimed, "This stuff is good!"

Calli said nothing, but kept on eating.

With the dish now empty both kittens were lounging on the passenger seat.

Clutch purred, "What was that stuff?"

Calli replied, "My Brenda-human called it 'crabmeat.' I think it's a special kind of cat food because it comes in cat food cans."

Clutch asked, "Should we tell them how good it is? Maybe we can get it all the time."

Calli hissed, "They're not smart enough."

"I don't know," replied Clutch. "My Pete-human seems to understand."

Calli growled, "Don't you know anything? Those are just tricks humans are taught. They don't even know how to bathe properly! They stand under water and rub themselves. We cats are much smarter!"

Clutch answered, "Maybe they know how to do human things and not cat things. On my farm the lead cow, Boots, told me 'Cows know cow things, and cats know cat things.' Maybe humans only know human things. She said her humans know their places and they take care of animals. Different animals have different ways, and we just have to all learn how to live together."

Calli snorted, "I think humans have to be told what to do."

Clutch decided it would be a good idea to change the subject.

"Why does your Brenda-human call you Calli?"

She snorted, "Because I am a calico! That means many colors. Aren't I the prettiest cat you've ever seen?"

Clutch said quietly, "No. My mother is. But you are very pretty. You look like my blanket. My Pete-human calls it a patch quilt. He says his mother made it for him when he was a kitten, and it was stitched together with love."

Calli growled, "I look like a blanket? I don't think I like that! My mother said I was the most beautiful girl in the world. Of course I'm the only one that lived. Do you have any sisters?"

Clutch replied, "I have one brother and four sisters."

Calli changed the subject. "Why does your Pete-human call you Clutch?"

Clutch replied, "Because I like trucks and want to drive. The pedal my Pete-human saw me standing on is called a clutch."

Calli inquired, "So what kind of cat are you?"

Clutch shrugged and answered, "I'm a farm cat."

"Well, if you ask me," chided Calli, "I think you are a lap kitty. You know, a pet. I don't think pets are good for much."

Clutch growled, "I do lots of things. I guard the truck. I check my human's food to make sure it's safe for him. I even wear a watch so he doesn't miss appointments and to make sure he is never late."

Both kittens yawned sleepily. Calli rested her head on Clutch's shoulder and whispered, "Even if you are a lap kitty, you still make a good pillow."

Clutch yawned. "You make a good blanket, Patch Quilt, um, I mean Calli."

Both went to sleep.

So tell me Pete, do you always carry dress clothes in the truck?" asked Brenda.

Pete laughed, "I sure do. I was a Boy Scout—always be prepared. When my dad drove, he always carried dress clothes, that way when he was not home for Sunday church he could still dress right and go to chapel at the truck stop. What about you? You're dressed to the max."

Brenda chuckled, "Girl Scouts. Same motto. If you had been at the safety banquet you'd recognize the dress."

Pete smiled and softly said, "No woman could be more beautiful than you are tonight."

Brenda blushed.

"I see they have sparkling red grape juice." Pete nodded to the waiter and said, "One bottle of sparkling red grape, please." He then turned to Brenda and said, "All the benefits of champagne with our dinner without the alcohol."

The waiter returned to their table bringing their beverages and glasses. He informed them, "Your meals will be ready in about 20 minutes.

Since they were the only customers at that late hour, Pete gently suggested, "Shall we dance?"

Brenda blushed yet again. "Yes. After all, we have time and music."

After their dance, they saw their waiter bringing their food. They then returned to their table.

Brenda asked, "Mr. Dobsin, where did you learn to dance so well? And don't tell me you learned that in the Boy Scouts."

Pete went silent for a moment and looked into Brenda's eyes. "My mother taught me every dance she knew. She said she wanted me to be ready for my high school prom."

Brenda's eyes widened, "For your prom? Tell me about it."

Pete grew quiet, "It was not what I expected. I had asked a girl in my class three months ahead of time. On the night of the prom I washed and waxed my father's new car and picked up my date. We went to the school gymnasium for the prom. After a dance or two, she informed me that she and her friends, along with her new boyfriend, were going to another party. My parents would want to know why I was home so soon so I went to Uncle Bill's instead. Uncle Bill and Aunt Mae never asked any questions. We stayed up until about 11:30 enjoying popcorn, hot cocoa, and old reel-to-reel movies. My folks were none the wiser."

Brenda put her hand on Pete's. "I hope your dates have gone better since then."

Pete looked at her warily. "Before tonight, there were no other dates, only work and family. So how was your prom?"

Brenda answered, "I went to a small private school. Prom wasn't a factor."

Realizing the warmth of Brenda's hand, Pete closed his around hers. After a few moments their gaze broke. Pete turned his head and sighed. "I guess we need to get some shut eye. New Jersey is still a long way to go." Pete paid the bill and left a generous tip.

They walked slowly across the parking lot, hand in hand, to their trucks. At Brenda's truck, Pete gently squeezed her hand and said, "Thank you, Miss Kingman, for the best date I've ever had!"

She replied, "And thank you, Mr. Dobsin. Perhaps we should do this more often."

Pete boldly looked into Brenda's eyes. "Miss Kingman, I do believe you are correct." After another long silence Pete said, "I guess I'd better gather up my partner."

Brenda was quiet as she opened the door.

Pete broke the silence. "I hope Clutch was a gentleman."

Brenda stepped up into her seat and, over her shoulder motioned for Pete to climb up. "Come up here and see this."

Pete wrapped his arm around Brenda's waist so neither one would fall. Together they looked at the kittens sleeping together on the passenger seat.

Clutch had his front paws around Calli, and her nose was nestled into his neck. They smiled.

Brenda said, "Let's not wake them. Let him stay until morning. I'll feed him."

Just then Calli's face brushed against Clutch's, and she nestled her nose into his neck."

Brenda sighed, "Oh, look Pete. Their first kiss."

Purely on impulse, Pete turned his head and placed a quick kiss on her cheek.

Brenda was clearly startled.

She looked at Pete who boldly said, "I won't explain, and I won't apologize. Just tell me one thing Brenda. Did I do it right?"

Brenda looked at him with a grin and asked, "First kiss?"

Pete turned about three shades of red. "No. I've kissed before. One I liked, then there was Aunt Mae, Mom, a cousin once, and one I got beat up for."

Brenda asked, "And now?"

Pete answered, "I liked that one very much."

Before Brenda could respond Pete kissed her hand, stepped down from the truck, and said, "Call me on the CB when you're up. We can get some breakfast and burn some day light."

* * *

The next morning, Brenda called Pete on the CB. "How about you, Lone Wolf? Are you out of your den yet?

Pete keyed his mike. "Yeah, Daddy's Girl. Let me put on a shirt, and we'll be ready for some wake-up juice." Pete met Brenda between their trucks and asked, "How's my partner this morning?"

Brenda smiled, "He and Calli are still out of it. I gave them plenty of food and water, but I could use some food myself."

They turned and walked toward the truck stop. Just outside the door, Pete stopped and looked at Brenda. "Thank you for last night. I had the best evening of my life. And about that kiss, I won't apologize.

Brenda softly smiled at him. "I'd slap you if you did. Now let's go get us some grub."

Tom Kingman walked into Rob Wendover's office, poured himself a cup of coffee, and sat down. After he downed his hot, satisfying drink he reached into his pocket and flipped a single key onto Mr. Wendover's desk.

Rob asked while looking at him, "Are you sure you want to do this? You still have plenty of good years ahead of you."

Tom smiled and said, "Bobby, take a gook look at that shovel nose in the glass case out there. When your father bought that truck, I drove team with him. When he started buying new trucks, he offered me a partnership. I turned him down because I'm a truck driver. Bobby, I bounced you up and down on my knee before they invented disposable diapers. For too long I've been driving trucks, for too long I've been leaving out. And for too long I've been promising my wife a honeymoon. Now you understand why they call me 'Too Long.' I'm gonna go home and be a full-time husband. Let's face it. I've been talking about that vacation with Phyllis for too long. I'm going to plant begonias, feed gold fish, and sit on the porch with my wife to catch every sunset I can."

Rob looked at his life long friend and said, "You best go home and pack. You leave out tomorrow.

Tom frowned and exclaimed, "You just don't get it, Son! I'm retired."

Rob reached into a drawer and pulled out a large envelope. He laid it in front of his friend. "Oh I get it Uncle Tom. It's just that I promised Dad I'd take good care of you. It's all there in the envelope; plane tickets, cruise ship reservations, ten days at a beachfront hotel, and $3000 party money. That's for you and Aunt Phyllis. Now get out of here before we get wet spots all over these tax papers. Millie has a new set of luggage for you. I had Jimmy put it in the back of your pick-up. You better get out of here before the two of you miss your plane."

Tom stood there looking at the envelope. He embraced his nephew and said, "You've been like my own son since your dad's death. Thank you."

As Tom Kingman left Rob's office he stopped in the driver's lounge for one last cup of coffee. Realizing the wetness on his cheeks he mopped his face with his shirtsleeve. With a quivering voice he said to the other drivers, "I sure wish they'd fix the A/C in here!" As he turned to leave he checked his pigeon box and found it unnaturally full. He pulled out his mail and found a large number of notes and cards congratulating him on his retirement.

Just then all the office personnel and other drivers converged in the lounge with a large cake and coolers full of drinks. Desperado, the yard man, looked at him and gruffly said, "We couldn't let you leave without a party Too Long."

Millie Wendover and her daughter Connie quickly loaded down a table full of snacks. They gave their Uncle Tom hugs.

Rob walked into the lounge and cleared his throat to get

everyone's attention. "I have a letter, written by my father, that I'd like to read."

He removed the letter from his shirt pocket and read,

Dear Tom,

You stuck by me through the worst of times when I bought my first truck. In the toughest of those years you even declined pay for a week or two at a time. When business started booming, I offered you a partnership. Again you declined. You said you just wanted to drive.

You stayed with me through everything. You were even the best man at my wedding. You were there when my first son was born as well as the rest of my children. Tom, you were my brother and best friend before you married my sister.

If you're hearing these words from my son, it's because I can't be here for your retirement. Tom, I've put 10 cents for every mile you've driven in a trust fund and entrusted my son to continue to contribute that same amount.

I've gone on to be with my wife in death. Now it's time for you go on to be with your wife in life. Enjoy the rest of your life, Tom.

Your friend, brother, and brother-in-law,

Bob Wendover

When Rob finished reading the letter, no one had dry eyes. Rob looked to his uncle and declared, "Do you realize that, up to this very last trip, you have driven 7,410,279 miles? Do the math yourself, Uncle Tom."

The two men embraced and everyone cheered and shouted.

Pete and Brenda traveled most of the day without speaking. Both were left to their own thoughts.

Pete finally broke the silence. "Hey Daddy's Girl, got any plans for dinner?"

Brenda asked, "What did you have in mind?"

"Well, I know a place in Amarillo. It's kinda showy, but the food's great. Maybe we can split a 5-pound steak or somethin'."

Brenda replied, "I know where you're talking about. I've always wanted to try that place. I hear they even have a free limo service for the drivers. Let's call it a date."

Pete suggested, "Let's dress western tonight, and dinner is on me."

Brenda responded, "Then a date it is. Tonight, let's see what we can find in the goody bag for the kittens. I think I have just the thing for dinner for the little ones. I have a can of shrimp."

Pete chuckled. "Why don't I break out a battery powered candle, so they can dine by candlelight?"

Brenda laughed.

Pete asked Clutch, "Hey Partner, how are you hitting it off with Calli?"

Clutch meowed.

Brenda started to speak when her 'check engine' light came on. She called, "Pete, I need to check the engine."

Pete answered, "There's a parking area 2 miles ahead. Can you make it that far, or do we need to go to the shoulder now?"

Brenda replied, "The parking area will be fine."

* * *

They pulled into the parking area.

Brenda shut her truck down and got out. She shut her door and then opened the hood.

Pete walked over and offered to help. "What's wrong?"

Brenda answered, "I just need a gallon of coolant. She's going through a gallon every 3 or 4 days. My new truck should be in by the end of this run."

Pete inquired, "How many miles does she have on her?"

Brenda replied, "She'll have a million miles by the time we reach Jersey."

Pete whistled. "She's got a lot of miles on her. Do you think she'll make it?"

Brenda smiled, "Of course she will. I have my fingers crossed." She added a gallon of coolant to the reservoir. "That should do it," she said. "We'll check it again when we stop at Amarillo."

"Do you want to do anything about lunch?"

Pete responded, "There's a small fuel stop at Tucumcari, New Mexico with all kinds of food around it. We can grab something quick to hold us over until our date, er, dinner."

Brenda squeezed Pete's hand. "I kinda like the word 'date.' We should use it more often. As for Tucumcari, burgers-to-go sounds good."

With her truck running fine now, they continued east, stopping only long enough to get a few burgers to eat on the run.

Upon arriving at Amarillo, Pete suggested that the kittens should dine in his truck, which Brenda accepted. She then insisted on providing a can of tiny shrimp.

Pete chided, "You know, Aunt Mae would frown on the kittens getting so much people food."

Brenda laughed. "What did they get on the farm?"

Pete replied, "Fresh cream, table scraps, um, never mind."

* * *

After fueling and getting the kittens ready for their date in Pete's truck, they headed for the showers.

Pete came from his shower wearing jeans, a white western shirt with red roses embroidered on the shoulders, and his boots, polished and shined.

When Brenda came from her shower she was wearing a knee length denim skirt, a beige cotton shirt with roses embroidered on it, and her boots, also polished and shined.

They both laughed about the roses. Pete's shirt was a product of Aunt Mae's handy work. Brenda proclaimed that she had done her own.

Pete and Brenda strolled hand in hand into the restaurant. The hostess proudly exclaimed, "It's not every day husband and wife dress to compliment each other! You two are the best pair yet." She took their picture.

Pete stammered, "Well ma'am, we're, I mean…"

Brenda quickly intervened by throwing her arm around his waist and saying, "Smile pretty dear. Would you take another one for us please?"

Pete's smile was one of shock.

Brenda whispered into Pete's ear, "No explanations, just fun, and nothing to be embarrassed about."

They were promptly shown to their table.

Clutch and Calli crowded around the food and water dish, devouring this new stuff called 'shrimp.'

"This stuff is great!" shouted Calli.

Clutch agreed with his mouth full. After they had eaten their fill, the kittens busied themselves by playing with Clutch's toys.

When Calli grew tired of playing, she glanced around the strange new truck and said, "You have a nice shed Clutch."

He replied, "This is not a shed. It's a truck. We live in trucks."

Calli snapped back, "Cats live in sheds."

Clutch answered, "Some do, Calli, but we live in trucks."

Calli didn't like being contradicted, but rather than argue, she changed the subject.

"Who are they?" she snapped looking at a picture on a shelf in the truck.

Clutch looked at the picture and answered, "They are my Pete-human's Aunt Mae and Uncle Bill.

Calli blurted, "They don't look too evil, but they're still humans."

Clutch was insulted that Calli had spoken so harshly of the humans that he had grown to love.

Since Pete had put Clutch's blanket across the passenger seat,

Clutch jumped up there and lay down to listen to the soft music that was always coming out of the radio.

Calli realized she was being ignored so she just lay down beside him on his blanket.

After a long while, Clutch asked Calli, "Why do you dislike humans so much?"

Calli glared at him and replied, "They're evil. They're bad. I had a human once who was with my mother. He dumped us out at a rest area. Somebody dropped some food. When my mother tried to get it for us to eat, a car ran over her and she died. That's why humans are evil. They abandon cats and kittens. They run them over with their cars and leave kittens to starve."

Clutch placed his paw on her shoulder and whispered, "They're not all that way. Your Brenda-human rescued you from the rest area and gave you a nice home and plenty of food. She even loves you. I don't think that's evil or bad. On the Dobsin farm, animals can be punished for hurting other animals. I saw Aunt Mae-human even swat Scrappy the dog with a newspaper because he got too rough with a kitten. Uncle Bill-human scolded Scrappy and told him he won't have a nasty animal on the farm, he better shape up. My mother, Miss Tabby, says, 'We all work together.' Even Boots the lead cow says, 'Every animal is obligated to do their share and then some.'"

Calli meowed, "And just what is expected of cats?"

Clutch replied, "We chase away rats and mice of course. My mother is the best mouse chaser on the farm."

Calli asked, "What do they chase mice for?"

Clutch answered, "Mice eat crops and the cows' grain and bring disease."

Calli inquired, "What do cows do?"

He replied, "They give milk and cream to the farmer."

Calli was on a roll. "What do dogs do there?"

Clutch puffed his chest and raised his head high. "Dogs warn the farmer when strangers come and chase bigger animals like rabbits from the garden and deer out of the fields. Usually, dogs just make a lot of noise."

Calli retorted, "I don't like farmers. They like dogs. Dogs are bad and they smell funny."

Talking about life on the farm made Clutch feel homesick. "You'd like Drowser. He's old and likes it when the kittens climb all over him. He even lets them bite his ears and pull on them. Even Della is nice to cats. She just had five puppies this spring. Scrappy, he's a stray that some one dumped out. Uncle Bill-human said he could stay as long as he's nice. Scrappy is okay, but sometimes he plays a little rough. My Aunt Mae-human whacks him with the newspaper to remind him."

Calli exclaimed, "Tell me more about these humans."

"The one my Pete-human calls Uncle Bill rides around on this metal thing he calls a tractor and makes things grow. He goes into the barn and puts buckets under cows and they fill up with milk. Boots, the lead cow, reminds him to give us kittens cream every time he milks. If any animal gets sick he and Aunt Mae make them get well. He even cleans up when they make a mess. They don't use a litter pan. The one my Pete-human calls Aunt Mae turns cloth into clothing and cooks food. We can smell it. She grows things to eat in what they call a garden. She also takes care of the smaller animals, too. When they're ready to have babies, she helps them to deliver.

All of my siblings and I were born in her kitchen. It was the same thing with Della's puppies. Animals that do their work properly have a good life. When she cooks she makes extra so the cats and dogs can have some too. Every time they walk by us, they say kind words and scratch our ears. Nobody works harder than those two humans. We love them very much."

Calli looked at him suspiciously for a long moment. "It all sounds good, but I'd have to see it for myself."

Clutch looked at her with sorrow. He realized she had not come from a home like his. "I will ask my Pete-human if you can come and visit our farm."

Calli snorted, "Don't bother. He won't understand."

The two kittens fell asleep.

* * *

A few hours later, Pete and Brenda returned to their trucks. Both were sleepy and overfed. After a few swift thank yous and goodnights it was decided it would be best for the kittens, who were resting peacefully, not to be disturbed.

* * *

Before leaving out the next day, Pete and Brenda thoroughly inspected their trucks as they always did. Pete asked Brenda, "Is your truck gonna make it?"

Brenda replied, "The coolant is only down a quarter inch. I have plenty if we need it."

Pete gave Brenda a long look and stated, "I guess we're ready."

Brenda put her hand on Pete's shoulder, "I'm running with good company. I'll be fine."

There was a long silence as they looked deeply into each other's eyes.

Pete broke the silence. "Where do you think we should stop next?"

Brenda replied, "We can easily make Memphis in 10 hours. That's a good spot."

Pete agreed.

Brenda insisted, "It might be a good idea if we stop along the way and restock groceries. Since you treated me to dinner two nights in a row I'll cook tonight. I won't take no for an answer."

Pete smiled. "You won't hear me argue. I guess we better get going."

They traveled most of the day with idle talk. Neither one wished to betray the feelings they had for each other.

Pete keyed his mike and asked, "Where do you want to stop for your shopping break?"

Brenda replied, "About 55 miles inside the Arkansas state line is a huge store with plenty of truck parking. They've got just about everything you could want there. Lone Wolf, do you still carry the charcoal grill in your stash box?"

Pete replied, "Absolutely. Why would I give that up?"

"Good," said Brenda. "We'll need it tonight."

Pete could hear the smile on her face.

Just then Pete's phone rang. It was Aunt Mae. "Hi Aunt Mae," said Pete. "Is everything alright?"

"We're fine," she replied. "We haven't heard from you for a few days. I thought I'd better check up on my boys."

"Sorry I haven't called," Pete blushed. "I've been running with another driver and I guess I got a little distracted."

Aunt Mae inquired, "Someone from your company?"

Pete boldly replied, "Yes. I'm running with Brenda Kingman. We both loaded out of Fresno going to the same place in New Jersey. She's having a little trouble with her truck. I'm going to follow her all the way."

"That's absolutely wonderful!" exclaimed Aunt Mae. "Of course, not that she's having truck problems. I know you two are behaving yourselves. You know Dear, her grandfather's farm is just over the hill from here."

"I promise you Aunt Mae, we are behaving," replied Pete.

Aunt Mae suggested, "Dear, you should bring her out to the farm sometime."

Pete blushed again. "I'll keep that in mind Aunt Mae. I know you would never do anything to embarrass me. I really do appreciate your concern, but right now I don't know if I'm even ready to settle down. Don't forget that I have this new truck to pay for."

After a brief silence, Aunt Mae softly said, "I'm sorry. I shouldn't meddle. It's just, since your parents' accident, you're the only family Bill and I have left. We both see you as being our own son. We promised your Mom and Dad that if anything happened, we'd take care of you."

"I know," sighed Pete. "No man could ever ask for a better family than I have. I love you Aunt Mae. Oh. I forgot to tell you. Brenda has a new kitten."

"That's wonderful. We love you too, Peter," she replied. "It's kind of warm in here today. The sweat's just pouring off me. I better go."

Pete sighed again. "I better get going. I promise I'll call you Friday. I'm gonna take a couple of days off the next time I get through Indiana. Clutch sends his love. Well, 'bye now."

Pete called Brenda on the CB, "Sorry it took so long. I was talking to Aunt Mae."

"That's okay," said Brenda. "Dad called. He said Rob is giving him and Momma a retirement gift. They're leaving out tomorrow—flying out to California for a 10-day Hawaiian vacation. He said something about Mom in a grass skirt and he needed a new weed eater, HA!HA!HA!" Brenda laughed.

Pete sounded amused, "I did not need to hear that!"

Brenda exclaimed, "Alright you smart alec. They are my Mom and Dad."

Pete said, "Okay, okay. I stand chastised. Anyway, since no one is gonna be at your place after we finish our round, why don't you come out to the farm for a couple of days? I have your grandfather's 1-cylinder tractor fully restored. Besides, it's been a long time since Aunt Mae and Uncle Bill have seen you. They really would love it if you came."

Brenda replied, "That sounds like a good idea. We can talk about it later. Anyway, the store is just a couple of miles ahead. Hey, Pete, let's do ribs tonight. I'll cook it—your grill."

Pete exclaimed, "It sounds like a winner to me. How 'bout I chill some sparkling cider?"

Brenda replied, "It sure sounds good to me."

"While I'm at it, Brenda, I'll pick up some swordfish for the kittens. We can grill it and share it too."

Brenda teased, "Why, Pete, are you starting to think outside the box?"

Pete grinned, "I'm a Dobsin. No one boxes us in."

Brenda continued, "You may not get boxed in, but my dad sure knows how to corner you."

Pete answered, "Well Brenda, you sure know how to do a good job of that yourself sometimes."

Brenda chuckled. "That, my dear, is a Kingman trait."

They both laughed.

* * *

With the shopping done, and their day almost over, Pete suggested to Brenda, "We'll probably find parking on the north side of the highway in West Memphis. They have a big lot there. We shouldn't have any problem finding two spots together. I gotta warn you, though, this is a rough town."

Brenda answered, "Yeah, it's not one of my favorite places. It could be worse though. We could be stuck in Jessup, Maryland."

Pete nodded, "I know what you're saying there. Anyway, after we park I'll get started on the grill. Will we need anything inside?"

Brenda agreed, "It sounds like a winner. It won't take long to cook once the coals are ready. I think we have everything we need."

After they parked their trucks, as Pete started the grill, Brenda quickly seasoned down the cage of pork ribs, wrapped them in foil, and placed them on the heated grill along with four large, foil wrapped gold potatoes. She called, "Okay Lone Wolf, you're the time keeper. I need 35 minutes on each side."

"You got it," said Pete. "One question. What are we going to do for 70 minutes?"

Brenda smiled. "We could use that time to start training our kittens to use their leashes."

Pete asked, "Will the potatoes be done enough?"

Brenda answered, "Just like mashed potatoes in the shell."

Clutch, they're trying to kill us! They'll use these strings on our collars to hang us from the mirrors!" cried Calli.

Clutch reassured her, "No. They just want us to walk beside them. I've done this before. They'll take us into the grass and we can walk there. These are called leashes."

Calli yelled, "I don't want to wear one!"

Clutch smiled. "I don't much like them either, but my human says it will keep us safe. I think they're afraid for us." Clutch was silent for a second. "They don't want anyone to run over us. They don't want us to get hurt. Our humans do nice things for us. We should do nice things for them. It's kind of fun to walk beside them. It even looks like we lead them," Clutch grinned.

Calli replied, "I guess it's worth a try as long as it looks like we're in charge."

Clutch purred to himself.

After a while, Brenda set up a small folding table and took the food off the grill. She carefully unwrapped the swordfish steak Pete had bought for the kittens, flaked it out, and put out the pork ribs and potatoes for everyone to eat.

With everyone fed, Pete brought out an ice-cold bottle of

sparkling cider. After filling two throw-away plastic cups he handed one to Brenda.

He raised his cup toward Brenda and Calli and said, "To two lovely ladies."

Calli was startled by Pete's comment. For the first time without prompting, Calli purred and rubbed against Pete's ankle, showing affection.

As Brenda and Pete dined, the kittens frolicked playfully. Calli said, "You know, your Pete-human might not be so bad after all. And Clutch, you aren't so bad for a farm cat—not that I was wrong or anything."

Clutch smiled. "Our two humans really seem to like each other. Maybe they belong together like we belong with them."

Calli retorted, "You mean humans can own humans?"

Clutch replied, "I don't think humans own each other, they just go together—belong together. It's sort of like putting cream and coffee together. It makes it taste different, but better."

Calli growled, "I don't know anything about coffee. I do know my Brenda-human smiles when she talks to him on that box his voice comes out of. Yesterday she said, 'Whatever woman can sink a hook into that fish will have a real keeper.' I didn't know my human knows anything about fish. Then she then said something really strange. 'When he bites, it will be right where he wants to be, and he'll make a splash that will startle everyone.' I just don't know what that Pete-human has to do with fish."

Clutch was puzzled. For a bit he was silent. Finally he said to Calli, "My Pete-human said things like that about her too. Maybe they think each other are fish, but I think it means they like each other a lot. I do know that since they left the place they called California, Pete's been acting real funny. He even said he wouldn't mind wearing a collar if it came from her."

With the usual snort from Calli, she said, "I didn't know humans wear collars!"

Clutch and Calli just had to admit that their humans were acting strange.

The next day, as they were leaving West Memphis, Pete commented to Brenda, "We can keep it short today and take our break at Glade Springs, Virginia."

Brenda replied, "I'm sure glad these are light loads. I don't know how much more this engine can take. I just had to add another gallon of coolant."

Pete responded, "After this circle Rob should have your new truck in."

The rest of the day went well for them. Even the traffic was light going through Knoxville, Tennessee.

Later on that afternoon Pete suggested they should stop in Bristol, Virginia. He said he wanted to pick up some groceries, and he wanted to cook dinner. "I hope you like salmon."

Brenda replied, "Now there's something all four of us could enjoy."

That evening at the truck stop Pete wrapped up several potatoes and carrots in foil and put them on the grill to cook. Next he laid a long slab of salmon on the foil, cut a lime in half, and lightly seasoned the salmon with lemon pepper, lime, and fresh mint leaves.

After the carrots and potatoes were done, he put the salmon on the grill. "Just 10 minutes on each side," he said.

After everyone had eaten, Brenda declared the salmon to be the best she had ever eaten and asked, "Is that one of Aunt Mae's recipes?"

Pete replied, "Nah. I learned it from a driver and his wife that I ran with across Wyoming. They go by the handles 'Go Joe' and 'Coffee Bean.'"

Brenda appeared stunned. "That's were I learned to make the ribs! The same people! I met them in Temple, Texas. We ran to Hershey, Pennsylvania up from there. He sure loved his wife…and cooking too."

"When I talked to them they had just bought a home in Pennsylvania. When they left home they adopted a cute little kitten. They said they named him after his son-in-law."

Pete replied, "Yeah. They told me about that."

The kittens were curled up against one another lightly sleeping, over-stuffed on the fish.

The following morning brought majestic blue skies over the Appalachian Mountains. After Pete and Brenda saw to it that Clutch and Calli had food and water they treated themselves to breakfast and plenty of coffee. Pete could not stop himself from gazing into Brenda's eyes.

Finally Brenda broke the spell he was under. "So where do you think Rob will send us when we're empty?"

Pete took a long pull from his coffee to clear his mind. "I don't know for sure. I hear he has a new contract heading out of the fish markets. Right off the docks, I'm told."

Brenda giggled, "That ought to smell real nice."

They both laughed.

Pete downed another cup of coffee and tried to ask casually, "Have you given thought to coming out to the farm?"

Brenda sighed. "I'd like to, but I'm not sure what dispatch wants to do with me. I can't really do much with the shape my truck is in."

Pete sighed, "If you do come, feel free to bring swimwear. The ponds have all been cleaned and the fishing is great."

Brenda laughed, "If I remember correctly, I spent more time swimming your ponds than I did my grandfather's."

Pete grinned. "If you decide you don't like my ponds, Uncle Bill has three more."

"How long are you taking off?" she inquired.

"Probably about five days," he replied. "I'll need to cull out the calves to fatten them up for market."

Brenda teased, "If I do come, where will you have me stay?"

Pete went quiet for a long while. "You can take Mom and Dad's room. It has a private bath, and it's probably the cleanest room in the whole house."

Brenda was deeply touched by Pete's words. She did not know what to say so she gently placed her hand on Pete's. "I guess we had better get going."

Pete slowly nodded his head, casually reached over, and grabbed both checks, saying, "Breakfast is on me."

* * *

Back at their trucks, both faithfully inspected their rigs before leaving. After Brenda added another gallon of coolant they were both on their way.

Pete called to Brenda, "I'll be back with you in a few minutes. I promised Aunt Mae that I would call her today."

Brenda replied, "I'll call dispatch and find out what they want to do with us when we get empty."

Pete answered, "Tell Vonell I'll have two hours left today but I'll have to show a ten-hour break afterwards."

"Great!" said Brenda. "What do you have tomorrow?"

Pete stated, "I'll pick up eight tomorrow and ten on Sunday."

Brenda replied, "Yeah, that's about what I'll have."

"Okay," he said.

He called Aunt Mae as he'd promised he would. After the usual greetings, Pete and Aunt Mae talked about the way things were going at home.

Aunt Mae inquired about Clutch. "You're not giving him people food are you?"

Pete replied, "Well, sometimes I may give him a little fish or shrimp, maybe even a little crab meat." Pete blushed. "It's not like I'm feeding him chili and coffee at home."

"Well, you know, Peter, people food really isn't good for him. Haven't you read the book I gave you?"

Pete asked shyly, "What do you usually do with your table scraps each night?"

Aunt Mae changed the subject. "I wish you were here to see this beautiful rainbow Peter! We just had a much needed rain here."

Pete smiled to himself, "I love you. Oh, Brenda may be staying with us for a few days out on the farm. If she doesn't have to run she said she'd love to visit."

Aunt Mae asked, "Our place or yours?

Pete answered, "I thought it would be good if she stayed in Mom and Dad's room."

Aunt Mae added, "Should I get a few ladies together from the church for a cleaning party, Peter?"

Pete replied, "That won't be needed, and you don't have to worry. It's a big house and there will be nothing improper. I haven't forgotten my upbringing."

Aunt Mae said, "I'm sorry, Peter. I was way out of line."

After they talked a while longer there was a knock on Aunt Mae's door so they ended their conversation.

* * *

Pete called Brenda on the CB. "Hey, Beautiful, what did you find out?"

She stammered, "What did you say?"

Pete answered, "I said, 'You're beautiful,' and I asked 'What you found out.'"

Brenda exclaimed smiling, "Be careful Lone Wolf. Compliments can get you into a lot of trouble. Anyway, Vonell said she's working on two loads for us to go back to Indy. She probably won't have the information until about 2 o'clock. She'll send it over the Qualcom. She wanted to know when we'll reach our final destination. I told her we're making good time and we should be there by 8 p.m. She also reminded us these loads are drop and hook, and to make sure our bonus is in Wednesday's check. Rob sent us a job well done. I asked her about the other three loads. The two teams delivered this morning. Rain Man will be in about 10 p.m. It looks like everyone got their bonuses. Do you really think I'm beautiful, or are you just saying that?"

Pete blushed and answered, "Of course I do, Brenda. Have you ever known me to say something I didn't mean? Hasn't anyone ever told you that you're beautiful before?"

She replied, "Sure. Dad, Grandpa, and some guy I gave a black eye."

They laughed.

They both traveled on, letting the engines do the talking, for neither one knew what to say.

As they passed the exit for Raphine, Virginia, Brenda called to Pete, "Why don't we stop at Greenville to get rid of this old coffee and get some fresh."

Pete replied, "It sounds like a good idea to me. I sure could use a good stretch. We only have four hours to go from there."

Brenda answered, "Let's go for it then, and try to keep your son out of the coffee this time!"

Pete laughed.

* * *

When Pete and Brenda returned to their trucks, they both had messages waiting for them. Pete read his and turned to Brenda. He said, "It looks like we're getting sea food out of Trenton, New Jersey going back to Indy. We won't load until Sunday. Why don't we take an hour in Woodstock, Virginia to fill our coolers. We can camp out at Bordentown, New Jersey after we fuel."

Brenda smiled after looking at Pete long and hard. "It sounds like a good idea to me. Our two little ones will probably need a break. I told Rob about the coolant problem. We're both to take the loads to the yard and he'll have the yard man take them to the warehouse Tuesday."

"It sounds like a plan to me."

Brenda was still struggling with her emotions. She put her hand on Pete's shoulder and gently asked, "Pete, are you getting serious on me?"

Pete answered, "For the first time I'm totally unsure of myself. Brenda, I promise that, when I figure it out, you'll be the first to know."

Brenda looked deeply into Pete's eyes and said, "That's fair enough." To change the subject, "We better get down the road."

* * *

Four hours later, they pulled into the East Side Warehouse and parked. Pete and Brenda took their bills into the receiving office.

"Hey Pete! Hey Brenda!" called Crystal Blevins in receiving. "It's been a while since I've see you two. Vonell called me earlier to let me know when you would be in. Brenda, drop yours in door 3. Pete, you can drop yours in door 5. When you come back in for your bills I'll have a fresh pot of coffee ready. Your empty trailers are in the yard."

"Crystal," said Brenda, "Pete and I each have kittens now."

"Really?" said Crystal. "I'm so glad. They really do make the time go faster. You'll have to bring them in before I let you have your bills."

"We will," smiled Pete. "We're starting to get used to this."

Pete and Brenda spotted their loads in the doors and grabbed their empty trailers. After, they carried their kittens into the receiving office.

Crystal made a huge fuss over Calli saying, "What a beautiful kitten you are!" She then exclaimed to Clutch, "What a handsome cat you are! Pete, what all does he have in him?"

Pete smiled, "He's just an Indiana farm kitten."

Crystal disagreed, "Oh, I don't think so. He may look like just a cream puff now, but trust me. Look at his fur and ears. Pete, he's got a little wild in him. My husband and I have been sponsoring pet shows—dogs and cats—ever since we started this business. I don't care what you say his momma is, I'm telling you that his daddy has got some Bob in him. He's gonna be one handsome cat. Trust me on that. He's gonna get big. You can count on it.

"Brenda, your calico is absolutely breathtaking. What's her name?"

Brenda smiled. "Why, her name is Calli of course."

Crystal purred, "I've jut got to take their pictures! Edwin and I are compiling pictures for cat calendars. I guarantee these two belong in a calendar."

Pete and Brenda decided that it was okay.

Crystal took their pictures and said, "Let me pull some grab bags for your babies, after I take some pictures of them together." Crystal took more pictures after which she gave them their bills and grab bags.

"You two will have to give me your mailing addresses. When the calendars sell, we always send a little something to the owners and their pets. With the calendar contest we always send a prize check to whoever wins first, second, and third places."

Pete smiled, "I don't much care about prizes, though I am honored that you wanted to use our kittens. How much are the calendars? I wouldn't mind buying one."

"Oh no, dear. You both get two calendars for free."

Brenda asked, "Well, we appreciate that, but what do they sell for? We don't mind paying."

Crystal never lost her smile. "Honey, trust me. We sell them for

$85 a piece, and we can't print enough of them. We export pet products all over the world. Our calendars are our biggest sellers. Think about it Dear, a global market, and your kittens, I would wager, will be the hottest of all. We only print 1 million copies a year. Most are sold in advance."

Pete shook his head in astonishment. "Wow!" he exclaimed, "I mean, I never realized pet items were so big."

Crystal grinned, "If these two get the votes I think they will, I'm looking at the winners right now."

Pete just shook his head.

Brenda changed the subject. "We better get going if we're going to get a parking spot in Bordentown."

Crystal added, "When do you pick up next?"

Pete responded, "Not until 5 a.m. Sunday in Trenton."

Crystal countered, "Why not just stay here? This time of year we run around the clock. We have everything you need. There are showers in the restrooms, plenty of food in the break room, and we're right on the water in case you two want a moonlight stroll on the beach. Tonight is gonna be a full moon."

Pete looked over to Brenda for some kind of backup.

She smiled, "Pete, we have been pushing pretty hard. At least here we won't have to worry about someone running off with our goods. Besides, a walk in the sand might do us some good. It's too bad we don't have any swimwear with us."

Pete asked, "Crystal, do you mind if I fire up the charcoal grill?"

She smiled, "Do anything you want. There are five acres of blacktop and twenty acres of sand and stone."

Pete replied, "Thank you. That's very generous."

Crystal added with the same smile, "I'll even tell security not to patrol the beach tonight, just in case."

* * *

That evening after dinner, Pete and Brenda took Clutch and Calli for a walk, then let them play without their leashes. As the two kittens were playing in the wet sand, they noticed something crawling out of the sand. It was a crab.

Calli demanded from Clutch, "What is that thing?"

Clutch replied, "I'm not sure. I've never seen one before. Let's get a closer look."

Calli said, "That thing sure does look strange. Let's play with it."

Clutch exclaimed, "Calli, I don't think that's a good idea. It looks a little dangerous and mean."

Calli snorted, "You're just afraid, you lap kitty. I'm bigger than it is and I can take care of myself!" Calli started to swat at the crab as it danced side to side.

Suddenly the crab grabbed hold of Calli's right front paw.

"MEOW! Make it let go! That hurts!"

Pete saw what was going on, rushed past Brenda, and scooped up Calli and the crab.

Calli cried, "MEOW! Make it go away! Make it stop hurting!"

Pete quickly pried open the crab's claw, freeing Calli, then quickly checked her paw to make sure nothing was broken. He cuddled the kitten and reassured her that the 'big, mean crab' was gone.

Brenda was also at Pete's side comforting her.

Pete continued to hold Calli and stroke her back until she finally started to purr. Eventually he put her back down with Clutch.

Calli exclaimed, "That giant monster tried to eat me! Your Pete-human saved my life! Maybe he really does care."

Clutch laughed quietly to himself and replied, "See Calli, I told you. Not all humans are bad."

"You know Clutch," said Calli, "I might even learn to like him."

Clutch purred softly.

Brenda suggested, "Perhaps the kittens have had enough fun for one night. I think its time for these two to go to bed."

Pete asked, "Why don't you let her stay in my truck tonight. I'll open a can of something special."

Brenda agreed that it would be all right.

Pete put the kittens in his truck, opened a can, poured it into their food dish, and closed the door. He let the kittens have some privacy.

Brenda gave him a hug. "That was very sweet of you, the way you reassured Calli."

Pete replied, "I couldn't let that thing hurt her. She's sweet. Now about that moonlight stroll."

"By the way," said Brenda, "what did you give the kittens?"

Pete grinned and answered, "Crabmeat."

* * *

The moon was full as Pete and Brenda took their stroll in the soft, warm sand. After a while they sat on a large rock.

Pete asked, "Do you like fireworks?"

"Fireworks?" replied Brenda, "I love them. Why?"

"Well," returned Pete, "We're about to see some. There is supposed to be a meteor shower starting in about ten minutes. I heard about it on a nighttime talk show I listen to. Look, there's one now!"

They watched the meteor shower for over three hours. Sometimes it was so intense the whole night sky was ablaze with the red, gold, green, and amber colors.

In the coolness of the night air Brenda snuggled tightly to Pete's side as he wrapped his arm around her. Finally she said, "As long as I live, I don't think I'll ever have a night better than this."

"My dad told me once that he proposed to Mom during a meteor shower. They watched it together back home," said Pete. "They had spread a blanket in her dad's front yard. The whole time her mom and dad sat on the porch swing, her dad with a 12-guage on his lap. After she said yes Dad walked up to her father to ask permission. He gave his consent. The gun wasn't loaded, he just wanted to see if Dad was made of the right stuff."

They both laughed.

"Well," said Brenda, "It's getting late. We'd better get back."

* * *

The next morning Brenda woke to a pleasant smell in the air. Upon climbing out of her truck she found Pete hard at work on the grill.

Pete smiled at her. "I had a lot of thinking to do last night so I took another walk. As the tide left out I gathered up a few of these guys." He pulled back the cover on a bucket by the grill. It was filled with roasted crabs. Opening the lid of the grill he revealed two large sea trout. Pete said, "Wait, there's more. Look at this." He opened his small cooler and held up a baby sea turtle.

"Oh!" exclaimed Brenda. "He's adorable. Where did you find him?"

Pete answered, "On the beach this morning. He was a late hatch. The gulls ate a lot of them. I couldn't let them get him. I'll take him to the water after we eat. I wanted you to see him first. I was able to rescue eight others. I let them loose in the surf."

Brenda could not put words to what she was feeling for this man. She gave him a kiss and said, "I'll go with you to turn him loose." She held the creature up, looking at what she saw as a trusting, innocent smile. It would be hard to admit, but she was falling in love.

As Pete was taking the fish off the grill, Crystal and Edwin drove up in their car and walked over to Brenda and Pete. "Something smells good," said Edwin.

Pete smiled, "Just in time. The trout are done and the crabs are cool. Hungry?"

Ed replied, "You bet! Let me run inside and grab a bucket of ice-cold pop. We can take the food up to the building. We have an umbrella and table up there."

Brenda asked Crystal, "Are you working this weekend?"

She replied, "No. Dave and John are working the weekend crew. Besides, a quarter of a mile of the best beaches in the state—who wants to stay here on the weekends? Actually, I told Edwin about your kittens and he wanted to see them for himself. I brought something for you two." She handed Pete a pair of blue and red swim trunks and Brenda a 1-piece swimsuit. She glanced back at Pete when she told Brenda, "With your figure, this should help hook that fish."

Brenda blushed.

At the table everyone started eating.

When Pete pulled a crab out of the bucket, Calli shouted, "MEOW! Monster!" and hid behind Clutch. Peeking out she said, "Look, they're eating them. I love your Pete-human. He caught and killed every monster in the sand last night."

Clutch rubbed his nose against her neck and said, "That smells like the divine stuff in our dish last night. And look, they're putting some in our dish!"

Calli snorted, "Sweet revenge! Let's go."

After spending much of the day enjoying the beach, they made their goodbyes.

They arrived in Bordentown, New Jersey for fuel and made it to the shipper in Trenton around 11 o'clock p.m.

Mike, the dock foreman, gave them their door assignments and reassured them they would be loaded early. They would be underway by 5 a.m. He said, "You two get some sleep. I'll wake you when you're loaded. Set your reefers at -20 degrees. This isn't pet food."

Pete suggested they drop down I-95 through Philadelphia, Pennsylvania onto I-76 to US 202 and US 30, and then take Route 283 into Harrisburg onto I-81 to I-70. This would save $25 in tolls. On Sunday morning there would be very little traffic except for Amish families in horse-drawn buggies on their way to worship.

Brenda agreed. "I've taken that way a few times myself."

By the time they reached Gap, Pennsylvania, Brenda noticed her engine temperature slowly rising. She called Pete. "Pandora is starting to warm up. There's a truck stop about 12 miles ahead at Lancaster. I think she'll make it that far."

Pete replied, "Okay, let's go through and check her out. Didn't you just fill her this morning?"

Brenda answered worriedly, "Yes."

CLUTCH THE TRUCKING CAT

At the truck stop, Brenda left her truck running while they checked for leaks.

After a few minutes Pete yelled, "Brenda, I found it! Shut her down!"

Brenda turned off the engine and walked around to where Pete stood. She asked, "What have we got?"

Pete replied, "You're leaking at the water cut off valve to the heater."

Brenda called the shop at their terminal to report the problem and line up the repair.

Marvin, the head mechanic was in. He asked, "How bad is the leak?"

Brenda answered, "Not too bad, but—..."

Marvin said, "The truck stop at Carlisle will be short handed on Sunday. Let me make a phone call, and I'll call you right back."

A few minutes later Brenda's phone rang. The mechanic inquired, "Can you make it to New Oxford, Pennsylvania? It's only 40 or 50 miles away. We have an account there. They can get you in tonight. The also have the parts on hand."

She replied, "We can make it there by 10:30 a.m. Thanks, Marvin."

Marvin answered, "You're welcome. Now get to it."

81

At 10 o'clock they arrived at the shop.

Paul Tillo, the mechanic on duty, looked the problem over and said, "The best thing to do with this thing would be to take the coolant cap off and put a new engine behind it. We'll have you out of here by 9 p.m. I have some other stuff ahead of you."

Pete asked, "Is there anything to do here?"

Paul answered, "Hanover is about four miles away, plenty of food, movies, and there's always the mall. Gettysburg is about ten or twelve miles west. You know where York is. Welcome to Sleepy Town. With this truck though, I'd suggest a church. The thing needs a prayer or two."

"Aunt Clara!" stated Brenda. "I just remembered. Dad has an aunt who lives here. Excuse me Sir, do you know of a Clara Snider?"

Paul reached behind the counter and said, "Here's the phone book. If she's listed, I can tell you how to get there. Look folks, you seem like very nice people, but I really do have work to do. You can drop your trailers in the lot, it's fenced in, just please find something else to do."

Brenda looked up the phone number and dialed.

After a short conversation with her very surprised great aunt she hung up the phone. "Thank you Sir. I just talked to Aunt Clara. Pete, we can bob-tail in. I even have directions. Thank you very much for your help, Paul. We'll be back around 9 o'clock."

B renda!" cried Clara. "I haven't seen you since you were in diapers! Look at you! You're all grown up! How is Tommy? You look just like Phyllis! Who is this? My don't you look handsome. You must be Peter. Why are we all outside? It's cooler in there. I hope you all are hungry. I'll just take a pan of something out of the freezer. How does lasagna sound?"

"I'm sorry your Uncle Wes couldn't be here. He goes fishing on Sundays, you know. He usually leaves about 6 a.m. If they're biting we won't see him until after dark. I swear I see less of that man since he retired. You know dear, he still substitute teaches. So Peter, tell me about yourself."

Pete answered, "As you can see, I drive for a living and own my own truck. I also own a farm in North Central Indiana."

The aged woman replied, "That's nice Dear, but I wouldn't think you would have much time to farm when you're always on the road. I was raised on a farm myself."

Pete realized he was about to really get grilled and it had nothing to do with chrome.

"Tell me about your farm."

Pete replied, "I have about 400 acres. Half of it is in pasture. I keep about 200 beef cows. I mainly run them back and forth between two pastures to make hay to carry them through the winter. My farm is half the original family farm. My grandfather split it between his two sons when he retired."

Aunt Clara suggested, "That's nice Dear. So tell me about your parents. Does your father also farm?"

Brenda placed her hand on Pete's, "Aunt Clara, Pete lost his parents several years ago."

She replied, "I'm sorry. I really didn't mean to… Please don't think of me as an old crow."

Pete smiled, "It's okay. I really don't mind. My dad also raised beef cows and drove, Mrs. Snider. Mom would often travel with Dad. I was an only child. When I was stationed in Germany they had their accident."

"I'm so sorry Dear. It's not my intent to be rude. I hope I didn't offend you."

Brenda came to Pete's rescue. "Aunt Clara, just how many children did you and Uncle Wes have?"

She answered, "We had six, three girls and three boys. My oldest and youngest sons both drove trucks. My Jeffrey is the oldest and gave up the road about four years ago. He opened up a garage to repair trucks. He's somewhere down in Arkansas. My Philip and his wife drive team. They drive for some refrigerated company outside of Carlisle. I think they have penguins on their trailers."

Pete added, "I know that company. Those birds are called puffins. They're a rather large operation, pretty good people I here, and pretty particular about their drivers. I gave them a good look when I started to drive, but I wanted a company closer to home."

Aunt Clara said, "That's nice. Do you have a nice house on your farm, plenty of room?"

Pete grinned, assuming where this was going. "Ma'am, it has five bedrooms, two full baths, a good sized parlor, and a very spacious kitchen."

Aunt Clara exclaimed with a smile, "Well now, it sounds like plenty of room for lots of children, if you ever settle down. It sounds absolutely lovely. Brenda, the last I heard of Tom, he was still driving himself."

Brenda sighed with relief. "Dad just retired this week. He and Mom are in Hawaii right now."

"Oh, how wonderful! He finally got to take her on that honeymoon." Aunt Clara slyly added, "Will there be wedding bells for you two, or are you two just really good friends?"

Both Pete and Brenda blushed.

Pete recovered quickly and replied, "Brenda and I have not talked about marriage. We both have strong values. I assure you, when we find out what the weather holds we'll tell you. I'll let you know how the water is if we decide to drink from that cup."

Aunt Clara smiled as she came to her final conclusion about Pete. "Brenda, I'm so proud of you and happy you found a man like Pete. I threw my best ammo and the bullets just didn't stick. This man is a keeper. Pete, if the two of you get together, I know I'll never have to worry. Please! I don't like it when my cooking goes cold. What would you two like to drink with that?"

Everyone agreed on coffee.

* * *

After a delicious and satisfying lunch with more coffee, Aunt Clara showed a different side. "Pete, I've lived on a farm for most of my life. When my husband and I retired, we divided most of our assets among our children with the understanding, of course, that they could sell or trade their portions of land preferably within the family. My boys Jeff, Phil, and Wayne desired to live elsewhere. Our Ginny also sold her land. It went to their sisters Brittany and Angela. Our old farm is divided between the two of them now. Brittany owns the orchard portion and Angela owns the farm and pasture. With the help of their husbands they still run it as one piece. What kind of cattle do you run, Pete?"

Pete answered, "I run a Brahma/Angus mix. They're good hearty stock and gentle to work around."

"How often do you rotate them?" she asked.

Pete smiled, "I change them out every 8 years. This way I rotate about 50 a year. I change out my bulls every 3 years, so I change one a year. The bull calves are culled out in the spring and fall. I keep about 20 for steer. The rest are all marketed, and we put one, a 9-month old steer, in my aunt and uncle's freezer. And there is always plenty of water from two ponds and a stream."

Aunt Clara asked, "How about your ponds Son, are they fish filled?"

Pete replied, "Yes, ma'am. My big pond is spring fed. I keep trout in there. My small pond gathers all the runoff. It's warmer there so I keep bass in it."

The now-smiling woman said, "It sounds like a good operation to me. Brenda, does your mother still bake like she used to?"

Brenda grinned, "I don't think there are too awful many better than she is when it comes to that."

"Dear, before you were born your momma used to travel with Tom. We often sent them back fruit grown off our own farm after a visit. Does she still jar things like she used to?"

Brenda answered, "She still does occasionally, but she mostly freezes them now. They still grow most of their own fruit."

"Yes," said Aunt Clara, "things always taste better when you grow your own, and you don't have to worry about what's in it."

As the three were talking over coffee, a very tall man, about seventy years old and wearing a shirt that read, 'If you didn't make it, you don't need it!' walked through the door.

"Honey, if I had known we were expecting company I wouldn't have gone fishing. Who do we have here?"

Aunt Clara responded, "You remember my nephew Tommy Kingman, don't you? This is his daughter Brenda and her friend Pete. They both drive for Wendover. Her truck is being repaired here in town so they came out for a visit."

"Mercy," said the silver haired man. "Now I'm glad the fish weren't biting."

As Pete and Brenda stood, Uncle Wes exclaimed, "The last time I saw you, you were still wearing diapers and threw up all over my shirt. Good Lord! You're all grown up. It seems like only yesterday. You weren't much bigger than a bucket of bait. Speaking of bait, you look wonderful. Don't tell me you're a full-grown woman already. It looks like you've got a good catch here.

Pete, has my wife cut you up yet or has she been behaving herself for once?"

"Now Wes, you don't have to go on that way," said his wife smiling. "We've been having a wonderful conversation, haven't we kids? I didn't cut him up. I only weighed and measured him real good."

Wes gave his wife a hug and asked, "Has she set a wedding date for you two yet or has she backed off?" Shaking Pete's hand, he said, "You can shut that truck off and bring in those two dust balls if you want to."

Pete answered, "They were both sleeping when we came in, Sir. We didn't want to disturb them."

"Oh, bring them in for a few minutes if it's okay."

Pete walked out to the truck and soon returned with both kittens in his arms.

Once back inside, Pete introduced Clutch and Calli.

The older couple took one look at Clutch.

Wes said, "I believe this young fellow has a little bobcat in him. Look at his face and ears." He looked at Calli and declared, "Now she's the prettiest patchwork quilt I've ever seen."

Calli was most definitely not pleased and screamed with a spit, "That's calico, not quilt! I am a calico kitten!"

Aunt Clara laughed, "Dear, you've scared her. Give the poor kitten to me." She scratched Calli's ears while saying, "There, there Dear. Aunt Clara knows how to treat good kittens. Maybe these sweethearts would like some fresh cream. I think you've insulted this kitten's poor feelings calling her a patch quilt. There you go. The big man brought you something to say he's sorry. Didn't you, honey," she finished, leaning down to put Calli on the floor.

As Calli walked over to the dish of cream, it was obvious that Clutch was amused. Calli hissed to Clutch, "It wasn't funny! I heard the other man tell Pete your momma was 'Bob.' Should I start calling you 'Bob' too?"

Clutch answered, "Boots the lead cow had referred to the Great Cat of the Woods as a bobcat. I don't know if that's a title or he's a different kind of cat. I do know my mother speaks very well of him. He does look different from the rest of us—very different. And his name is not Bob. Maybe he's my father. He's much bigger than the other cats. His tail is short, and he has spots all over him. His fur is reddish brown. The neatest thing about him is the fur spikes on the end of his ears. He is so smart. I think he knows everything. Even Scrappy the dog doesn't mess with him. If he is my father, I hope I turn out just like him."

Calli mewed, "I don't even know if I have a father. My mother never told me where I came from. Do you think I could meet this Great Cat of the Woods someday?"

Clutch replied, "If you lived at our farm it could happen."

Suddenly the really tall man bent down and dropped two large shrimp to the kittens. Calli quickly smacked his hand with her paw, "That's for calling me a quilt!"

Clutch looked at Calli and inquired, "You're not still angry at him are you?"

Calli snorted, "Of course not. We cats have to train humans not to do some things, though. It's hard to be angry with someone who gives you cream and shrimp but we gotta let them know who the boss is."

Clutch shook his head. "Whatever you say Calli."

She added, "That Aunt Clara-human, cats have owned her before. She is very well trained, just like our humans are. With him, give me a week or two and I might be able to teach him a few things."

With their shrimp finished, Calli said to Clutch, "Now watch this." She walked over to Wes and placed her paw on his foot and meowed to him, "I want more shrimp."

The tall aging man looked at her, then at the dish and asked, "Is the shrimp all gone? I have a few more in my cooler. I'll peel them for you." After placing four more shrimp in the dish he added, "That's the last of them. I don't have any more."

Calli looked at Clutch, "See? If you tell them what to do, they'll give you the last piece of shrimp they have."

Clutch chuckled to himself as they gorged themselves on shrimp.

Back at the garage, the mechanic was just closing the hood on Pandora when Pete and Brenda arrived. "Okay lady," he said, "I replaced the valve and the hose going to it, but if you ask me, the whole truck is shot. Just sign here and you can leave. If you really want my opinion, I'd say park it somewhere when you get back and show it some mercy. Don't take her back out on the road."

Brenda smiled and thanked him. They both hooked up to their loads and moved on.

About forty-five minutes later, they reached Carlisle, Pennsylvania and jumped on the Pennsylvania turnpike.

Brenda suggested to Pete over the CB, "Let's stop for the night at New Stanton. We can finish our run to Indy in the morning."

"Yes," Pete replied. "If we get hungry we can finish off the food your Great Aunt sent out with us. I'm anxious to try her pizza noodle casserole."

Brenda said, "Those two really are something else, aren't they?"

Pete laughed, "I think they're absolutely wonderful. It must be great having relatives like them. I know we haul out of the turkey plant at New Oxford. All of those loads go to teams though."

Brenda shrugged to herself and said, "I guess that leaves us out. Anyway, Mom and Dad will be glad to know that they are okay."

"By the way, Brenda, did you write down their number just in case we get back through there?" asked Pete.

"Absolutely," she replied. "You did promise Aunt Clara you would call her," she laughed, "about that water."

Suddenly, Pete's voice was very serious, "Yes I did and I meant it. Anyway, there are two people I would love to stay in touch with. It must be great having such an extended family. I know my uncle has a few cousins, but I don't know where. I've never met them. I've only ever heard Aunt Mae speak of them."

Brenda smiled and said, "I have it right here."

* * *

Eight a.m. the following morning, Pete called to Brenda on the CB, "Rise and shine Brenda!"

She gave no answer.

Again Pete called, "Time to get up Daddy's Girl!"

There was still no response.

Pete felt reasonably sure that Brenda was still asleep and would not hear him. He softly said, "Brenda, I'm falling in love with you."

Brenda responded softly, "I know Pete. I feel the same way about you. I was just out of my truck kicking the tires. Let's talk over gourmet coffee this morning. My treat."

Pete choked on the words, "Uh, yeah, let's."

They went into the service plaza to freshen up and grab their coffee to go.

They sat down on a bench outside. For a long while, they sat in silence, looking at the cups in their hands.

Finally Brenda shattered the silence, "When did you first realize you had feelings for me?"

Pete, feeling like a scared little boy in a grown man's body, stammered a bit and expressed, "I…I…I think it was the day we were swimming in the pond and you had a cramp in your leg. I pulled you out. It was the first time I wrapped my arms around you. I think that's when I first fell in love with you."

Brenda looked surprised and exclaimed, "Pete! We were eight years old! You mean to tell me you've had feelings for me that long?"

Pete smiled sheepishly and replied, "I guess one never forgets his first kiss." He asked, hoping to avert the attention, "How 'bout you?"

Brenda profoundly blushed and whispered, "Same here."

With neither one knowing what to do or say, Pete wrapped his arms around her for a tender embrace and kissed her reassuringly. They held one another for what felt like almost an eternity.

Brenda whispered, "I don't want to, but we better get going."

Pete sighed, "Yeah, I guess we better."

As they turned to go back to their trucks, Pete embraced Brenda one last time. "Brenda, I love you."

She softly replied, "It sounds so much better face to face."

They had driven through Washington, Pennsylvania and then Wheeling, West Virginia before either spoke.

Brenda asked, "Pete do you really think it's a good idea for me to come out to your farm for a while? Aren't things kind of changed?"

Pete answered, "Absolutely. I think it's a great idea. It will give us a chance to talk. If you're not comfortable with me being in the house, I can always take a bed roll out and sleep with the cows."

Brenda laughed. "That won't be needed. I trust you. Even more, I trust myself."

Pete replied, "That that settles it. You won't even need to bring your fishing rods. I have plenty."

Brenda answered, "You know me Pete, I still prefer a long sycamore branch with a hook and string. Do you think your aunt will mind if I spend the days with her while you help your uncle?"

Pete exclaimed, "Mind? She'd love it. If you think your Aunt Clara is bad about questions, wait until Aunt Mae gets you in her kitchen."

Brenda laughed, "I can't wait. It will be good seeing her. I guess that settles it."

They had just cleared Columbus, Ohio when Brenda called back to Pete, "I'm starting to get a tapping noise from under the hood. It's not bad, but it's new."

Pete replied, "Yeah, you're getting smoke from your stack. How's your coolant level? Are you losing any oil?"

Brenda answered, "The oil is fine. It sounds like the rings to me."

"Let's try to nurse her in," said Pete.

Brenda agreed.

By the time they reached the 4-mile marker on I-70, Brenda called to Pete, "I'm starting to lose oil pressure!"

Pete responded, "There's a truck stop to the right at the state line. Let's get off there."

Brenda agreed, "Pete, her temperature is starting to climb. Come on, girl. It's not much further to go. One more mile. You can do it."

They eased off the parking area into the truck stop parking lot, by which time the engine was knocking profusely.

Brenda immediately shut off the engine and Pete raised the hood. With one look at the engine, he knew what the problem was. "There's less than 100 miles to go."

Pete called the owner of the company and informed him that the block on Brenda's engine was cracked.

After informing Rob of where they were he asked, "Pete, will it start?"

Pete asked Brenda to start the truck. When it would not start, he told Rob, "The motor is locked up. It won't turn."

After a moment of silence Pete's boss asked, "Can you bring Brenda in your truck? I'll ask Kathy to bring out the wrecker to bring in the tractor. I'll send Jim out to take the load over to the receiver using the yard truck."

Pete agreed to do that but suggested they should wait for the wrecker and the yard man. He said, "That way no one can steal any freight."

Rob agreed and said, "I want to see you two in the office as soon as you get in."

Pete replied, "Will do."

Pete put the dollies down while Brenda pulled the airlines and fifth wheel latch. Pete used a chain to pull the tractor away from the trailer. Brenda grabbed her logbook and put Calli over in Pete's truck while they waited for Kathy and Jim.

By 3 o'clock that afternoon Pete and Brenda were in the driver's lounge at Wendover Trucking.

They walked over to the dispatch window and Vonell informed them, "Rob knows you're here. He's with another driver right now. Good luck. He's not in a good mood."

About five minutes later, Rob stormed into the lounge with Woodrow Sykes, still arguing. "For the last time," yelled Rob, "I'm telling you, I can't afford to keep you on! The one time you were actually on time in two months and I'm stuck with fifty cases of top dollar T-bone steaks that spilled all over the floor because you didn't think it was necessary to use a load bar! That just cost $10,000 out of my pocket! I'm pulling your lease. You're fired!"

Woodrow roared, "Nobody fires Woody Woodpecker! I'll quit before I'm fired! I'll just take my truck and leave Wendy!"

"First off," shouted Rob, "don't ever, ever call me 'Wendy.'" Rob took a deep breath then calmly said, "I don't care if you quit or are fired. Please leave. I don't care. Just go."

Woodrow stomped out the door.

Still red in the face, Rob motioned Pete and Brenda back into his office. They both looked at each other and took a deep breath before following him in. Once inside his office he said without looking at them, "Take a seat. I'll be right with you." He placed both hands on the windowsill and slowly began to count. "1, 2, 3," Rob paused slightly, "8, 9, 9 ½." He then turned around and said, "Sorry about that."

Neither Pete nor Brenda wanted to know why.

"Pete, we have a problem. The good truck is down. Jimmy is using the spare. Brenda's new truck is already three months overdue, and the dealer tells me it's going to be at least another four to six weeks. I have two choices. One is to lay Brenda off."

Brenda braced herself and asked, "What is your other choice Rob?"

He looked at Brenda and did not answer immediately. "Pete, I need a favor. Either of you can say no if you want to."

Pete placed his hand reassuringly on hers then asked, "Have you ever known me to not want to help? For you and Brenda, you got it."

Rob replied without hesitation, "I don't want to lose Brenda as a driver. I'm not even going to bring up family ties. You two are the best of the best. Pete, I'm asking you to team with Brenda. Here's my offer. You get paid all miles, minus half her regular pay. I'll pick up the other half, all your road tax miles for this year, and half your fuel for as long as it takes to get her a new truck. I'll put that in writing if you need me to."

Pete looked at Brenda and gently asked, "What do you have to say?"

Brenda inquired while looking into Pete's eyes, "What about Buttons or City Girl?"

Rob answered, "Buttons married Crowbar last month and they're driving team. City Girl was in an accident three days ago. The truck's totaled. She's gonna be at least nine months on the mend." Rob shook his head. "Pete, you're the only driver I can trust. Brenda's the best driver in this entire company—better than the best, and I don't want to lose her."

Neither Rob nor Pete noticed that Brenda was returning Pete's affection when Max, a large orange cat who was missing his right ear, bounded onto Brenda's lap from Rob's desk.

Pete smiled, "I've got a lot to do at the farm and I won't be back until Monday, but I'm game. Brenda, what do you say?"

Brenda laughed and finally said, "It seems that Max thinks it's a good idea." She smiled and added, "Let's do it."

Rob sighed with relief and exclaimed, "Thank God! Something finally went right! Uh, sorry folks." Rob leaned back in his chair, feeling more relaxed. "Pete, if you need help with the calves, give me a call. I might could bring out my sons Saturday if you need us."

Pete replied, "We should have it wrapped up by Friday. If I can't get in a bull hauler we might need to stay another three days."

Rob nodded his head.

"Brenda, do you want me to find you something to do while you're waiting? I'll pay you hourly and put you up in a motel if you would like."

Brenda gave Rob a smile that he had never seen before and replied, "I'm gonna stay out at Pete's farm. I think some time off would do me some good—get back to my roots—however long it takes."

Only then did Rob realize that Pete and Brenda were holding hands, openly displaying mild affection. As Brenda's cousin, he wanted to ask questions, but if anything was happening, he would find out soon enough. "Okay," said Rob. "Brenda, I'll get your truck, and it'll be dressed out like I promised. Pete, don't think I'll forget this. Thank you. Now, what to do about fifty cases of T-bone steaks? Sorry folks, enjoy your time off." He smiled at his cousin and added, "Don't enjoy it too much. I need you both back."

Brenda looked down at her hand in Pete's and, without removing it, looked back at her cousin with a smile. "Come on Pete. We're off duty."

When they left the office Brenda turned to Pete and said, "Here comes Krazy Kat with Pandora. I'm gonna go clear her out and take the stuff to the house. While I'm there I'll pick up a few things for out on the farm. I guess I just want to say goodbye to Pandora."

Pete smiled. "Why don't you let Calli come home with us? Clutch will keep good watch over her."

Brenda punched Pete on the arm, "You two bachelors looking after a girl? It reminds me of a movie that I saw once as a kid."

Pete replied, "Yeah, I remember that one, and it turned out fine."

Brenda kissed him.

"If it'll be much past 9 o'clock when I get there I'll call and just come out in the morning."

Pete replied, "I'll be up late anyway, writing out checks. If you feel up to it, just come on out."

Brenda agreed. "I'll see you later."

Pete added, "Clutch will probably want to see his mother. Do you think it would be alright to take Calli over to Uncle Bill's?"

Brenda laughed. "Is old Drowser still around?"

Pete smiled, "Yeah. I think he'll be around forever."

She continued to laugh. "He's the babysitter for kid or kitten. Go ahead. By the way, how old is that mutt now?"

"He's got to be at least twenty. I'm out of here Girl. Goodnight."

Brenda added, "Oh! Are we going to be using horses or pick-ups?"

Pete called over his shoulder, "Do you think you can still handle the reins?"

Brenda gave a 'thumbs-up' and a nod of her head. Then she was gone.

Pete unhooked his trailer and turned to the kittens. "Come on you two, time to go to the farm."

Calli screamed to Clutch, "Where's my Brenda-human? Pete abandoned her at that truck place! He's stealing me! I want my Brenda!"

Clutch sighed, "Its okay. Pete is not stealing you or abandoning Brenda. We're going to the farm. Your Brenda-human will come out tonight. If she didn't trust Pete, you wouldn't be here. Besides, you'll get to meet my family. Isn't that wonderful?"

Calli snapped, "And just how do you know this?"

Clutch replied calmly, "They've been talking about it for a couple of days. Don't you remember?"

Calli glared at him and answered, "Oh yeah, that. Well if she's not there tonight, I'm going to bite Pete… And maybe you, too."

Clutch shook his head and sighed, "Whatever."

* * *

A little over an hour later Pete turned onto a state road, then onto a gravel lane that led back to the Dobsin Family Farm. As he did his turnaround at the milk shed Uncle Bill and Aunt Mae emerged from the house to welcome their nephew home. Pete climbed out of his truck with both kittens in his arms.

Aunt Mae hurried over to give him a hug and a kiss. She then looked down at the kittens and exclaimed, "Good Lord, Bill! He leaves out with one kitten and comes home with two."

Pete answered, "This is Calli, Brenda's kitten. I told you about her."

Aunt Mae exaggerated, "Bill, she's beautiful. She looks like she got caught in the middle of a paintball free-for-all."

Uncle Bill added, "I don't know, she looks pretty enough to be one of your patchworks."

Calli was just about angry enough to spit.

All of the animals on the farm gathered to welcome Clutch home.

Pete set the kittens down and told Clutch, "You two run along. I'm sure your momma wants to see you. Clutch, be a gentleman and show Calli around."

The kittens started to trot off to the waiting welcome party until Calli suddenly stopped. She was overwhelmed by all the strange animals she had never seen before. She realized that she was very afraid.

Clutch stood by her side and purred, "It's alright. These are my friends and family. You don't have to be afraid."

Calli growled, "I'm not afraid!"

From the midst of the group walked a tall, proud female cat that commanded respect. She strolled up to Clutch, and affectionately purring, rubbed heads with him. "Welcome home

Son. We've missed you very much. I see you brought home a young lady."

Clutch purred, "I love you Mother. This is my friend Calli."

Tabby sat down smiling. "Hello Calli. Welcome to our farm. I am Tabby, the head mouser and, as you know, Clutch's mother."

"I'm…I'm…I'm Patch Quilt, um, I mean Calli," she stammered in awe.

"Well Calli, you may call me Miss Tabby. Now come kittens. We'll introduce Calli to all of our friends and family."

The kittens followed her affectionately.

Tabby led them into the center of the group.

Immediately all of the animals started firing off questions all at once.

Tabby simply sat up straight and everyone fell silent. "I'm sure the kittens have much to talk about, but they've just arrived. Let's give them some air and be patient. Let them talk when they're ready."

Clutch walked around to his littermates and rubbed noses with them. He then returned to his mother and said, "I've seen so much. I just don't know where to begin."

Tabby gently prodded, "Tell me Son, what is that around your neck?"

Clutch replied, "Miss Brenda-human gave this to me. My Pete-human can look at it and know if he can make it to a place on time. He wears one on his paw too."

One of his sisters asked, "So Brother, do you eat chili?"

Clutch replied, "Sometimes we eat shrimp, crab, and just a few days ago, we had swordfish. I have eaten chili, though."

Another one of his sisters asked, "What's wrong with Calli? Did the Great Cat make a mistake? Does anyone know what color she's supposed to be?"

"No." declared Tabby. "She is a calico. They are very special and rare. She's the most beautiful one I've seen. I bet there's not another one like her. She's a gift from the Great Cat. You children are all very privileged to see a beautiful calico. There's something else. I've been told there's never been a male calico. We are all so blessed to have Calli with us. I'd guess the Great Cat is a calico, representing all."

All of the animals looked at Calli with awe. Calli rubbed herself against Tabby's legs in thanks.

Tabby smiled down at her. She said, "Now since there are so many animals I'm going to introduce you to all the clan leaders. This way, as you wander about our beautiful farm they can introduce you to the individuals of their clans." She led Calli up to a chicken and said, "This is Miss Penny."

Calli lowered her head to show respect. "I am pleased to meet you ma'am."

Miss Penny simply tilted her head to one side and replied, "Pleased to meet you too, too, too. I, my dear, dear, dear, am in charge of egg production."

Next Tabby introduced Miss Cecilia to Calli adding, "She is the head ewe."

Calli replied, "Pleased to meet you Miss Cecilia"

Cecilia bowed her head and baaed, "I am the head of wool production, and the head sheep. I am responsible for all the ewes, the female sheep."

Tabby then introduced her to Miss Della.

Miss Della barked, "Pleased to meet you Calli. My job here is to train the puppies for security so everyone is kept safe."

Calli looked at her with awe. "Everyone needs protection from whom?"

Della replied, "There's a lot of protection needed. Sometimes from wild dogs, deer, rabbits, and even the human element. Young teens might vandalize, and there are others who may kill or steal. I teach my recruits to never trust a stranger."

Calli meowed, "Are there lots of wild animals?"

Della barked, "Some with four legs and some with two. Now run along Calli. I'm sure Tabby has other department heads to introduce you to. And I have rounds I need to make."

Tabby led Calli out to the pastures. Before long they were standing in front of a large cow.

"Miss Tabby," mooed Boots. "I understand your kitten has returned from his travels. Is all well? Who is this young lady?"

Miss Tabby bowed to the huge animal. "Miss Boots, all is well with my son."

Boots replied, "Please do understand why we did not come to welcome you, but you know how it is with us."

Tabby only nodded and smiled, "Calli, this is Miss Boots, the lead cow. She is in charge of milk production. She and her ladies are responsible for about half of this farm's income. Milk production is very, very important here."

"That's right," declared Boots. "There is a large variety of foods that are made with milk."

Calli bowed deeply. "Clutch tells me you're the wisest animal on the farm."

Boots mooed again, "Although I'm usually right, I was very wrong about that kitten. Please bring him by when you have time. I must apologize. You two run along. The girls and I have much milk to produce."

Tabby turned to Calli and said, "I believe we have done enough for one day. Now I'll bring you back with the rest to meet my family and by then it will be time for us to take our naps."

The Dobsin family was just finishing dinner.

"Aunt Mae," said Pete, "Thank you so much for cleaning up around the house for me. I appreciate all that you are doing for us."

"Peter," she replied, "I was quite glad to do it. I must admit it was a little hard for me to go into your mom and dad's room. That bedroom needs sunshine. Besides, all I needed to do was change a couple of sheets, put fresh blankets out, and spruce up the kitchen a little. I just hope you two have a fun visit." Aunt Mae used her drying towel to dab at her eyes.

"Well," he sighed, "I should grab the kittens and head back home."

Aunt Mae firmly protested. "No Dear. Let them stay here. I know Tabby will take excellent care of Calli. It will give the two of you a little bit of time alone together."

"Yeah," interrupted Uncle Bill. "They'll be fine. I'm sure Brenda won't mind. Besides, it will do Calli some good to be around other animals."

Pete replied, "I guess it would be okay."

Aunt Mae added, "Here Pete, take this along with you, just in case you two get hungry. I prepared extra. Now get. You don't want to leave that girl waiting for ya'."

Pete hugged his aunt. Uncle Bill walked him out to the truck, but first they took a moment to check on the kittens. Calli was curled up tight against Clutch's chest, sound asleep with Tabby close by.

The two men smiled.

* * *

Back at the truck Uncle Bill asked, "Son, when do you want to start culling calves?"

Pete answered, "The truck is ordered for Saturday but you know how that goes. If we start Thursday we should be done by Friday afternoon."

Bill asked, "Are we going to use horses or pick-ups?"

Pete smiled, "When have we ever used anything but the horses?"

Bill laughed. "You know some people like the change. Me? I like it the old way."

Pete nodded, "I'll call Jeff and Tom Pierson."

Uncle Bill replied, "They're good hands. They've cut calves since they were in diapers. Anybody else?"

Pete answered, "Yes. I'll stop by the Zook Farm to see if Amos and Abraham are available. Those two Amish men are first rate help, two of the hardest working men I know."

Bill said, "I hope you and Brenda have a wonderful time. We've known her family for years. They don't come any better. You're a Dobsin. I know you'll never forget it. Pete, I hope things go right for you. That's all I'm going to say. Which mount are you going to chose for Brenda?"

Pete replied, "That's a tough call. I think Ginger would be best. I'll ride Buck."

Uncle Bill agreed. "I haven't decided yet. I'm leaning toward riding Joe. I'm going to hire out the milking for those two days—take it easy. Those two boys know this spread well. They know the chores."

Before Pete left Uncle Bill added, "Son, I will see you in the morning at around 4 o'clock sharp."

After a quick hug, Pete left.

At about 7:45 that evening, Brenda called Pete on his cell phone. "I didn't want you to think I changed my mind. I'm about fifteen minutes out."

Pete responded, "That's alright. You said it would be about 8 o'clock. Just in case you're hungry, Aunt Mae sent food over for us."

"Great! I didn't grab anything from town. I wanted to get out here."

Pete asked, "What would you like to drink?"

Brenda inquired, "Do you have any fresh squeezed cow juice?"

Pete answered, "Of course! It doesn't come any fresher."

At exactly 8 o'clock Brenda knocked on Pete's door.

Pete opened the door and smiled. "I'm really glad you're here."

Brenda gave him a hug and said, "Me too."

Pete said, "I'll bring in your bags for you. Dinner will be ready in about five minutes. Brenda, I left the kittens over at Aunt Mae's. They were resting so peacefully, I didn't want to disturb them."

Brenda smiled. "That's fine. I'm sure Clutch won't let anything to happen to Calli."

Pete replied, "I better put dinner out for you." Pete took the cover off the serving tray to reveal a large portion of roasted beef, along with roasted carrots and potatoes simmered in buttermilk. "I hope you're hungry. Aunt Mae sent enough for an army."

Brenda replied, "I hope you'll be eating with me. I can't eat all that."

Pete exclaimed, "Then dinner for two it is!"

After dinner, Pete went to clear the table.

Brenda stopped him. "You took care of dinner. I'll take care of the dishes. Go take care of something else. I've got this."

Pete replied, "You don't have to."

Brenda responded, "You did tell me to make myself at home didn't you? I'm doing it. I'm making myself at home. Now get!"

Pete replied, "Yes, ma'am!"

Pete quickly slipped out onto the front porch and sat down on the swing. Propping his feet up on the banister, he was totally immersed in the magic and charm of the last rays of the sunset.

After a while, Brenda joined him and brought some coffee along. She was wearing a long flowing nightgown made of strips of satin. She was displayed in the light of the full moon and he could clearly see the colors of the rainbow in the cloth.

It was difficult for Pete to speak. He finally expressed, "Brenda, you are so beautiful. Where did you ever find such a lovely nightgown?"

Brenda smiled and put her hand on Pete's. "It was given to me as a gift." She whispered, "Your mother gave this to me."

Pete remembered seeing the same color materials in the sewing room and smiled, shaking his head.

Brenda explained, "While you were in basic training, I would visit my grandparents, but I always spent at least two or three hours with your mom. She gave this to me about a month before their…" Her voice broke, and she couldn't finish.

Pete could see the tears glistening in her eyes and gently kissed them away, holding her close.

She finished by saying, "This is the worst I've mourned them yet."

They held one another for a long while before she pulled away.

"We better turn in. Tomorrow will be a long day. If I remember correctly, the milking starts at 4 o'clock, right?"

Pete nodded his head.

"Then off to bed with you Pete."

He answered again, "Yes, ma'am!"

At 4 o'clock sharp, Pete followed his uncle out to the milk house. As soon as the coffee pot was started, the two men prepared the milkers for wash.

Over coffee, Uncle Bill asked, "Sleep well, Son?"

Pete smiled. "Like a rock, Uncle Bill."

He teased, "I thought you might sleep in today."

Pete laughed. "You know me Uncle Bill, I always did like to wake up the rooster."

All throughout the milking Pete worked with a zeal that made Uncle Bill sweat just looking at him. It was what Dobsin men did when they have something on their minds. When the milking was all finished the men walked inside for a bit of country breakfast.

During breakfast it was quite obvious that Pete was distracted. After all, he had barely touched his food. When he finally did, he put pepper in his coffee, syrup on his eggs, and ketchup in his oatmeal.

Uncle Bill leaned back in his chair and casually asked, "My, isn't the grass a lovely shade of purple today?"

Pete mumbled, "Yes it is."

Next Uncle Bill asked, "Do you think the Colts have a chance of winning the World Series?"

Pete responded, "It's too early to tell but they should."

Uncle Bill asked, "Do you think the Martians will deliver the milk on time?"

Pete answered, "I've never known them to be late."

Aunt Mae angrily interrupted, "What kind of nonsense is this? Purple grass? Martians delivering milk? And I most certainly know the Colts play football! Peter James Dobsin, what have you done to your food? Did you two get kicked in the head by heifers this morning?"

"What? Mae honey," cooed Uncle Bill, "it should be obvious to well trained eyes like yours that the boy is in love. I'd say he didn't sleep a wink last night and he even embarrassed Boots when he kissed her on the nose this morning. Yup! He's got it bad."

"Well it still doesn't justify what he did to my coffee. Pete, I'll make you another cup."

Pete gulped down the peppered coffee and got a strange look on his face, followed by a look of pure determination. He slowly finished his fresh cup of coffee without replying to Uncle Bill's statement.

"Uncle Bill do you need any supplies for the farm?"

He answered, "Well I could use a couple of gallons of teat dip. Just ask Harvey to put it on my account. How about you Mae?"

She replied, "I'm good to go. Peter, are you sure you're all right? But maybe you should take a nap before going into town." Her green eyes were now flashing and her hands were firmly planted on her hips.

"Well," said Pete, "maybe a couple of hours won't hurt."

"You're drunk Son, and it's nothing you've eaten or drank. Go sober up."

Pete nodded his head and went to lie down on the bed in the parlor.

At 12:30 Pete awoke. After a light lunch, and a kiss to his aunt, he walked the short distance home.

Brenda greeted him with a cup of coffee and explained, "I was over to see my grandfather this morning."

Pete asked, "How is your grandfather doing?"

She smiled, "He's okay. I fixed him lunch and we talked a bit. He said he was glad to hear Dad gave up his keys. He and Dad haven't talked much for a lone time."

Pete nodded.

"So what's the program for culling calves?" inquired Brenda.

He replied, "There will be seven of us, including you, on horseback. Uncle Bill is going to hire out his milking and barn chores for two days. Aunt Mae is going to keep the bean pot going. We should be done by 1 or 2 o'clock on Friday."

Brenda offered, "Pete, why don't I fix dinner on Friday evening for Uncle Bill and Aunt Mae? It will give her a break after all that cooking."

Pete answered, "That's a great idea. I need to go to town to pick up a couple of things. Uh, want to come along?"

Brenda replied, "I promised Grandpa I would take him to the cemetery this afternoon. How are the kittens doing?"

Pete responded, "They're fine. I think Tabby was teaching Calli how to hunt mice. I noticed Clutch showing off a couple of spots. By the way, Aunt Mae wants us to have dinner at her place so we can all discuss the details of the work ahead."

"It all sounds great to me."

After another cup of coffee Brenda handed Pete her shopping list adding, "If you have time would you stop by a jewelry store and pick me up a polishing cloth? I'll square it with you when you get back home." She held up her left hand to show off her grandmother's ring. "I didn't have time to do it yesterday."

Pete smiled at her looking at her ring. "It's a perfect fit." He said, "You know, I can get it cleaned for you today and still get the cloth. I'm going to be next door anyway." The tips of his ears were pink.

Without hesitation Brenda removed the ring and placed it in his hand. Then she kissed him. "I sure appreciate this. You don't know how much."

"Well," he said, "It will be a pleasure. I should be back around 5 o'clock. Should I meet you at Aunt Mae and Uncle Bill's?"

Brenda answered, "I'll be back here by 4:30. Meet me here and we'll walk over together."

He replied, "It sounds like a winner." He hopped into his pick-up and headed out.

Upon getting into town, he immediately went to Messinger's Family Jewelry Shop. Inside the store, he was greeted by an ancient man who looked at Pete for a moment. He smiled and said, "Petor Dobsin. Petor, I haf not seen you since you vere a little boy. Vat sort of ring? I haf all kinds. Es it for you?"

"No," said Pete. He was silent for a moment before he said boldly to the man, "I'm going to ask someone to marry me."

The aged man smiled and put his hand on Pete's. "Our Petor is getting married! Do I know her? Oye! Forgive an old man. Now vat do you haf in mind? No! Vait! Come sit over here. I vill show you my selection." The older man went to a safe, opened it, pulled out a tray, and placed it before Pete. "Let's see Petor. Zere are many, many rings, but only one for zat special person."

It did not take Pete long to locate the ring he wanted. It was a quarter carat, yellow diamond set in a heart, surrounded with several tiny rubies. Pete reached out and picked up the ring.

The elderly man smiled. "Zat vone come vith a matching vedding band. I show you."

Pete cleared his throat and asked, "How much are they Sir?"

The old man frowned, "Zat set is $3500. Ah, you know vat? Ve make it $3000, just for you. Any man's style ring free."

Pete looked firmly at him and asked, "Can you take a check?"

He smiled, "Yas, from you, anytime."

As Pete was writing out the check, Mr. Messinger added, "I make ze rings for your mozer and fazer vith my own hands. Ah, I need to know vat size."

"Size?" Pete reached into his shirt pocket and produced Brenda's ring. "This ring fits her perfectly."

The aging man's face lit up as he held the ring. "Ah, I know zis ring. I make it vith my own hands too. I make it for Thomas Kingman and hes vife 25th anniversary. Petor! Are you going to ask Thomas Kingman's granddaughter Brenda?"

Pete smiled.

"Here. Let me clean zis ring quickly. Zis ring is size six. Give me your hand. I see vat size you need. Size fourteen. You pick up prize ring, I pick up yours. Come back at 4:30."

"I'll be here," replied Pete.

* * *

Pete hurried next door to the farm supply store and picked up a few things for himself and a 4-gallon supply of teat dip for his uncle. He then went to the grocery store to fulfill Brenda's shopping list. He also made sure to grab several bottles of sparkling grape juice.

* * *

At 4:30 sharp he returned to the jewelry store.

The German man had him try on his ring.

It was a perfect fit.

Mr. Messinger placed the rings in three boxes and said, "Remember ze red box is her grandmozer's ring. Ze black box is ze new ring."

It dawned on Pete, "What if she says no?"

The jeweler said with concern, "It vill be fine. Trust me, it vill be fine."

Pete then remembered, "Do you have any polishing cloths?"

The ancient man smiled, "Here, I give you three. So tell me Petor, how is it you haf zis ring to give me size?"

Pete blushed, "I told her I would get it cleaned and polished for her."

The old man laughed loudly, "And you haf done so. Haf you ask her yet?"

Pete shook his head no.

"Ah," said the elderly man. "You know, ven I marry my Gretchen, I trick her to vere she ask me. People do not pay me for advice. I sell fine jewelry, so advice is free."

Pete laughed.

"I know you both since you vere children. I vould love to vatch you put vedding ring on her hand. Forgive an old man for being bold. It vould give my heart great joy to be a part of young people's happiness, even if all I did is sell a ring. You go now. I am sure you have more important zing to do zan spend many hours vith an old man."

Pete shook his head smiling and said, "Thank you for everything Mr. Messinger, and I mean everything."

On his way home, Pete stopped at the Zook farm and was greeted by the eldest of the family. "Petor, it is good to see you. It has been a long time. My sons and I are on our vay to milk so I can not give you much time."

Pete nodded his head. "I'll keep this short. I do not wish to detain you. I have come to ask you, if your sons are not busy for the next two days, I would like their help culling calves. As always, they will be well fed and well paid."

Mr. Zook turned to Pete and said, "They vill be there. Vat time do you vant them?"

Pete inquired, "Will 7 o'clock interfere with their chores here?"

He answered, "No, ve vill milk half hour sooner. If not done, the girls can finish help milking."

Pete nodded his head, "I'll have them both back to you by 4:30."

Mr. Zook replied, "So long as you have them both back by 5. Vork them for their full day. You alvays pay them for it. They are goot young men—honest men. It is goot ven they vork for you. You do not corrupt them. You are a goot neighbor as your family alvays has been. Petor, tell Villiam it vould not be a bad thing to see him and his vife. They are goot people and alvays velcome, as you are. Goot day my friend."

* * *

Pete hopped back into his pick-up and, on his way home, called the other men to confirm that they would also be working for him for the next two days. He finished his conversation as he pulled up in front of the house. Out of the corner of his eye, he noticed something that caught his attention—the wash lines were full.

"I hope you don't mind," called Brenda. "I gathered up all the dirty laundry out of the hampers. I did not go into your room."

Pete smiled, "I do have a dryer, but thank you."

Brenda chided him, "Yeah, I saw that thing beside the washer. I just figured, they'd smell a little better in this wonderful breeze."

"I love you," replied Pete.

Brenda smiled. "Dear, I'm starting to get used to hearing that. I like the way it sounds."

"Oh, I have something in my pocket for you." Pete produced her ring.

Brenda held out her hand, so he could slide her ring onto her finger. He teasingly kissed her hand.

* * *

"Mae, Pete and Brenda will be here at any time. I think it best we hold our tongues when it comes to talkin' or when it comes to askin' questions about them. As much as we can, let's talk about how good Calli gets along with the rest of the farm animals."

"William Dobsin!" scolded his wife, "You make it sound like I've no sense at all, that I would even try to meddle. Honey, let's face it. There's nothing we would love more than to see that boy marry off. Especially to the granddaughter of old Tom Kingsman. You know, his family has been in this county even longer than ours."

"Well," said Uncle Bill, "if it makes you feel better, I'm a little antsy myself. You remember Pete's prom night?"

"Yes," replied Aunt Mae. "Poor Peter looked like he was carrying a ton of bricks on his shoulders."

Bill said, "He really wanted to ask Brenda."

"Why didn't he?" exclaimed his wife. "They only lived thirty miles away!"

Bill laughed softly. "It would of torn him up if she'd said no. That boy has had feelings for her for a long, long time. He was afraid if they did get together and they had a spat it would destroy the friendship they've had for so long. If you ask me, I'd say Brenda is his first and only love. He needs a real catch. He goes out of his way to avoid the young women when he's home, even at church. I believe that boy would eat a load of manure and pick his teeth with the spread bars if she asked him to."

"Bite your tongue, Bill! Don't talk that way. Besides, he'd probably have to put salt on it first!"

They both laughed. "No more talk. They're here."

Just then there was a knock on their door.

* * *

As the two men stood on the back porch talking over their days' events, the women busied themselves by readying the table.

"Pete, I hope this afternoon went better for you than this morning."

Pete slowly nodded his head. "Oh yeah, that reminds me. I picked up four gallons of teat dip. We walked over and I didn't bring it, but I'll bring it over tomorrow. Do you want me to bring it over to the milk house early so your hands have it?"

Bill replied, "Nah. There's no big hurry on it. I have ten gallons of it in the store room."

Pete looked surprised.

Uncle Bill smiled. "Son, I figured you needed an excuse to get into town. It seemed you were real anxious to have a reason to go. You've got enough vaccine in the barn refrigerator to take care of 500 calves and enough paint sticks to color all your calves like they're wearing tie-dye t-shirts. I'm not gonna ask your business. I just gave you a good excuse to go into town."

Pete gave his uncle a hug.

With that Aunt Mae opened the door and summoned everyone in.

They all took their places and joined hands while Uncle Bill asked the blessing for their meal and family. They dined on some of Aunt Mae's finest at the laden down table. They enjoyed meatloaf, salad, broccoli, home jarred corn, and, of course, her prize-winning bread and butter pickles. For dessert they chose from apple, cherry, rhubarb, and chocolate pudding pie. While they ate, they engaged in conversation about the work ahead. It was well understood that Aunt Mae was prepared to over feed a small army. The others would work together to cull out the bull calves, except for the ones that still nursed, one herd at a time. At no time were whips or prods to be used. Of course there were none to be found on the farm anyway.

Brenda volunteered to help Aunt Mae with breakfast.

Aunt Mae agreed to that, but insisted that she would need no help with lunch.

Bill and Pete would handle the shots as the calves were loaded onto the trucks.

Over the course of the next two days, the seven people on horseback segregated 147 bull calves. Aunt Mae cooked food that was so delicious even the Zook brothers brought no food from home.

Friday morning Pete received a call on his cell phone to inform him the trucks would not arrive until Sunday morning at 8. Pete told them that he was busy until noon therefore the loading would not start until about 1 o'clock.

After Aunt Mae cleaned up after the luncheon meal, she would return home and make a hearty meal for her wranglers.

Thursday evening Brenda reminded Pete that she would like to cook for Aunt Mae and Uncle Bill.

The invitation was gladly accepted.

By 1 o'clock Friday afternoon all of the calves had been neatly penned. After the horses were returned to the barn Brenda excused herself to start the preparations for the next meal.

When Pete and Uncle Bill were finally alone, the elder of the two commented, "Son, you haven't had a lot to say over the last couple of days, but you've sure been smilin'. Anything you want to tell me about?"

Pete answered, "Have you ever known me to tip my hand and show my cards? Uncle Bill, just give me a couple of days and you'll see how things are going."

It was not a normal thing for him to keep secrets from his uncle, but Bill Dobsin would not pry. The Dobins were honest people and never said anything that they did not mean.

After Aunt Mae had finished cleaning up from lunch, she decided to spend a portion of time with Brenda at Pete's house. She, being a proper farm wife, always brought a gift. She was bringing Brenda a fresh dozen eggs and a jar of blackberry preserves. She had just left her kitchen and was walking across the yard when Scrappy came running over and bumped her hand, sending the eggs crashing to the ground, breaking every one. Aunt Mae strongly scolded him.

After cleaning up the mess and putting the basket on the porch she continued on to Pete's house.

Brenda already had a cake in the oven and was preparing a roast to bake when Aunt Mae knocked on the door.

Aunt Mae said, "I'm sorry Dear. I was bringing you fresh eggs but that nutcase of a mutt Scrappy knocked them out of my hands and broke every last one. I don't mean to complain, but I think that dog is crazy." She laughed a little then added, "Quite truthfully dear, he's not crazy, we are. We let him stay."

As the two women sat down for tea, Mae let out a small sob and dabbed at her eyes. "I'm sorry. Vicki and I got together every afternoon for tea. It's been so long since I've had tea here. We couldn't have been closer than sisters. You'd think we had the same mother. It's been six years and I still can't believe she's gone. Your grandmother passed on not long after. She was such a sweet woman and a wonderful neighbor.

Brenda nodded. "I know what you mean. I lost two women I loved so close together. We all lost them. I can't imagine how it was for Pete and your whole family."

The two women embraced.

Brenda suggested, "Aunt Mae, Sunday afternoon, while the men are loading the calves, why don't we pick some wild flowers in the meadow and then go to the cemetery to put flowers on their graves? I've been waiting for a chance to spend some time alone with you anyway.

Aunt Mae looked at her for a long while and replied, "Child, I would love to. It's a wonderful idea."

A meeting was quickly called. All the animals of the farm met in the meadow.

Tabby was insistent that all of the kittens should attend. "Farm business is everyone's matter."

Even Drowser was in attendance.

Della ordered Scrappy, "Report to the center of the ring Pup! As part of security and other matters, it seems that our Scrappy knocked a basket containing 12 eggs out of Mrs. Mae Dobsin's hands and broke them."

Miss Penny cackled out, "Do you have any idea how much painful work it is, is, is to lay 12 eggs? That represents a full day of work for twelve of us. Twelve very beautiful, very precious eggs ruined, ruined, ruined!"

Drowser added in, "Pup, it seems there ain't a day that you don't cause trouble. Why don't you just behave?"

Roger, the head ram, bellowed, "Go back! Go baaack to where you came from!"

Boots quickly cleared her throat to speak, "I don't know about everyone else, but I for one would like to hear what Scrappy has to say. I do realize that twelve eggs are very important and this is the fifth incident this month, but please let him speak."

Scrappy laid on the ground whimpering.

"Now come along Dear," called Boots. "Talk to us. Tell us what's wrong."

When Scrappy could hold it no more he cried out, "I guess I don't belong anywhere. I was taken away from my mother when I was just a baby and given to a family. I was doin' real good there until one day when I tried to tell my master I needed to go out. He was busy reading his paper. I had an accident in his house. A couple of days later, he took me for a ride in his car and dropped me out in the middle of the road. He drove away. Then I saw all of you. I came here hoping to find a family. Everybody tells me, 'Scrappy, behave!' 'Scrappy, you're a fool!' 'Scrappy, you don't belong!' Nobody ever tells me how to belong or behave! All I ever wanted was friends, a family."

Calli walked up and touched noses with him. "All of those things that happened to you happened to me also. I don't know how long I'll be here, but I'll be your friend."

All of the other animals hung their heads in shame.

Tabby spoke up, "Scrappy has never done anything to hurt anyone. We all have been so busy with our own matters, not one of us tried to teach him anything."

Drowser barked, "Pup, hang out with me for a while and then, well, I'll teach you the rules."

Della added, "If you really, really, want to learn, I could teach you security. But, don't expect me to cut you any breaks."

Boots also added, "Scrappy, don't be afraid to come and talk to me or ask my advice."

Roger looked at him for a long while, "Maybe you're not so baaad after all. Don't lock horns with me though."

Penny chirped up, "Accidents do happen, happen, happen. I broke two or three myself."

Finally Tabby spoke again, "What do you think Scrappy? Will you give us all another chance?"

He barked, "Thanks. Thank you everyone." He then looked down at Calli, "Thank you for understanding. You really are quite nice."

* * *

As Uncle Bill and Pete were clearing the tack room Pete glanced at all the animals in the pasture. He asked, "Uncle Bill, what do you suppose all the animals are doing together?"

Uncle Bill chuckled, "It looks like some sort of farm council. Funny, they didn't invite us."

Both men laughed.

The elder man asked, "So what time do you want us there Son?"

Pete answered, "I believe Brenda said 6:30."

Uncle Bill was silent for a moment and then said, "It's been a long time since I've taken a meal in that kitchen," and let out a slight sniff. "It's been a long time since I've even gone to the house. It's going to be a special treat."

Pete smiled. "I'm going to take one last look at the calves then go get cleaned up for dinner. Uncle Bill?"

"Yeah Son?"

"I love you," Pete said.

The elderly man looked at him with watery eyes and replied, "I love you too Son."

At 6:15 Bill and Mae Dobsin knocked on their nephew's door. Brenda let them in and informed them, "Pete will be with you in a moment. He's finishing his shower." She was adding the finishing touches to the dining room table. "Dinner will be ready in a few minutes," she told them.

Pete came a moment later dressed in his casual khaki pants and a pale blue button up shirt.

Uncle Bill sniffed the air and said, "I don't know what that girl cooked, but it sure smells like your momma's food. Mae, honey, you're the best cook in the county, but I believe this girl might give you some competition."

Aunt Mae grinned. "Well, she had some of the best teachers."

A few minutes later Brenda opened the doors to the dining room. She entered the living room and invited everyone to dinner.

When everyone had taken their place at the table they joined hands. Uncle Bill was asked to offer the blessing.

With the blessing given, everyone helped themselves to the stuffed flank roast, fresh whole green beans, brussel sprouts in cheese sauce, cooked carrots, and for dessert, apple walnut cake—homemade of course.

After dinner Aunt Mae triumphantly proclaimed, "The meal could not have been better if I'd prepared it myself!"

Uncle Bill had been enjoying a third helping of cake when he inquired, "Mae, do you have this recipe?"

His wife replied with a smile, "No dear, I don't. And I don't want it."

Bill answered hastily, "Well, I guess she should move in. Wait a minute, Mae! You set me up. We agreed."

"Sorry Dear," she added with a sly grin.

Brenda and Mae cleared the dishes and put away the leftovers while Pete and Bill retired to the front porch swing. They said nothing and simply enjoyed being alive.

At about 8 o'clock the two men rejoined the women in the house. Pete suggested that they should all go to the parlor. After disappearing into the kitchen, he reappeared in the parlor holding a tray with four empty glasses and a bottle of sparkling cranberry juice.

After everyone was served Pete asked Brenda, "Have you ever played the word game?"

She replied, "No I haven't."

Pete countered, "We play it all the time here."

Having no idea what Pete was talking about, Aunt Mae started to protest.

Bill firmly grasped her hand and spoke over her enthusiastically, "Why don't you tell her how it's played?"

Pete's ears were now scarlet red. Despite Aunt Mae's mild anger and apparent confusion, Pete went on, "Well, you see, you form it as a question or an incomplete sentence. All you have to do is fill in the missing word."

Brenda innocently replied, "Sure. Let's give it a try. It sounds like fun."

Pete smiled and added, "I'll ask you about four or five questions to see if you get the hang of it."

Brenda agreed.

Pete started with, "This is the document you have when planning your estate."

Brenda replied, "Will."

"Okay, a female sheep is called…"

Brenda answered, "Ewe."

Pete nodded his head. "Who had a little lamb?"

Brenda said, "Mary."

Pete quickly asked again, "What is the third note on the musical scale?"

Brenda quickly responded, "Mi."

At that point Pete immediately dropped to one knee before her and produced a ring from his pocket and declared, "I thought you'd never ask."

Brenda slowly recovered from her shock and asked, "What is the opposite of no?"

Aunt Mae and Uncle Bill shouted out together, "Yes!" Their eyes were filled with tears of delight.

Bill smiled and proclaimed, "Yup! He's a Dobsin!"

At about 9:45 Uncle Bill yawned and stretched. He reached out his hand to his wife and said, "Dear, milkin' starts at 4 a.m. I don't think the girls will understand if I oversleep. I don't think I can stand anymore excitement tonight anyway."

Pete gave his aunt and uncle both one last hug. He said, "I'll see you and the ladies 4 o'clock, Uncle Bill."

His uncle gave him a sly look. "I'll understand if you're not there."

Aunt Mae glared scornfully.

Pete held Brenda close to his side. "Oh no, Uncle Bill, not until we're married."

Brenda gave Aunt Mae a confirming nod that set her aging heart at ease.

They left out for home walking across the garden.

Drowser reminded Scrappy, "Now do it the way I told you to, Pup. Go in at a trot. Keep them in sight, come to a walk beside them. Don't jump up, don't rub them, and don't act like you're happy just to be there. Whatever you do, don't get between them. This is your chance! Go! Now!"

Scrappy, remembering what old Drowser said, did exactly what he was told as Uncle Bill and Aunt Mae neared the porch.

Mae smiled down at Scrappy and gave him a pat on the neck. "You're such a good boy, Scrappy."

He let out a 'yip' and trotted off into the darkness.

On the porch Bill wheeled his wife around in his arms and kissed her tenderly.

Aunt Mae exclaimed, "What was that all about?"

As they opened the door and entered he whispered, "We'll talk about it inside."

Scrappy quickly reported back to Drowser. "She called me a good boy!" he barked excitedly. "Drowser, what does it mean that Pete popped the question?"

"What do you mean, Pup?" he growled.

Scrappy replied, "Miss Mae kept talking about a ring. She

used the word wedding and the way Pete popped the question."

Drowser responded, "Pup, this sounds real serious. You better go wake Boots. Tell her I told you to wake her. I'll summon all the department heads. There won't be time to get everyone."

* * *

"Miss Boots! Miss Boots! Wake up!"

She warned, "Pup, you just woke me up. This better be important."

"I'm sorry, but Drowser said to wake you. He said he's calling an emergency meeting of all the department heads."

Over the next few minutes the animals arrived.

Miss Penny clucked, "I was sleeping, sleeping, sleeping! This better be important. You didn't break another egg did you, you, you, Scrappy?"

Drowser let out a long howl and everyone fell silent. "Some events have come to my ears and I feel they require immediate attention. If my information is correct, it means great things for this family and this farm. It seems Mr. Peter has given Miss Brenda a ring and has, I quote, 'popped the question.'"

Boots was instantly alert. "Drowser, please repeat this. I want to be sure. How did you get this information?"

"Well, I was coaching Scrappy on the proper way to walk with the Dobsins. This is the report he brought back to me. Better yet Pup, why don't you tell them," commanded Drowser.

"She patted me on the neck and called me a 'good boy!'" he yipped happily.

Tabby quickly added, "We're all happy to hear that, but tell us what else she had to say." She encouraged gently, "Tell us the part about this question."

Scrappy said, "Miss Mae got wet at her eyes talking to Mr. Bill about how beautiful the ring was, the strange way he popped the question, and then something about preparing for a wedding."

Again the animals all started shouting at once. Finally, Boots let out a long bellow. All the animals looked around at each other. "You see Scrappy, our council gets all of its information from what we overhear from our human partners. It appears our very own Pete Dobsin has asked the young woman, Brenda, to join our family as his wife."

Drowser barked, "Yup, that's my take of it too."

Tabby added in, "In the daylight hours, let's all be extra attentive and gather as much information as we can. Tomorrow night, we'll discuss what we've heard. I'm sure Mr. Pete and Miss Brenda will tell Clutch and Calli themselves. After all, they will be more affected by this than we are. I'm sure they will come to us immediately."

Miss Penny cackled, "Gossip, gossip, gossip, I love, love, love it!"

"Okay," mooed Boots, "The council is adjourned. Everyone back to bed."

* * *

Holding true to his word, Pete arrived at the milk house at 4 a.m. Uncle Bill smiled at Pete, "Did you sleep well Son?"

Pete answered, "For the first time in a week, I slept like a rock—in my own room of course. As you can see I brought your dip."

Both men laughed out loud.

"How long have you been carrying this on your chest?" his uncle inquired. "What I mean is, when did you know that you were in love with her?"

Pete looked at him strangely for a minute and replied, "It all goes back to when she and I went swimming and she cramped up."

Uncle Bill let out a long whistle. "Good Lord, Son! That's been eighteen or twenty years!" Suddenly he realized, "That's why you never dated. That prom thing was a disaster! You didn't date because you had your heart set on her. I gotta hand it to you, Son. Now that's what I call determination. Well, let's get the milkin' done."

Usually, each man used four milkers at a time.

In between cows, Pete asked, "When did you realize you loved Aunt Mae?"

Uncle Bill laughed. "Now there's a story for ya'. Mae Harris was a city girl. They moved here from the Chicago area while her father continued working the city. While we were in the third grade I put a frog down her back to make her squeal. Instead, she just fished it out and said something about boys not knowing how to take care of pets. She said she'd keep it for herself. I figured a girl who could handle a frog the way she did was all right by me. I guess that, like you, I fell in love about the same age."

Both men laughed and neither noticed that every time they spoke the cows closest to them would stretch out their necks trying to catch every word.

"Tell me Son, have you two set a date?"

Pete replied, "Rob wants us to team for a while, but I don't want us to leave out without being husband and wife. I wouldn't care if we got married today. Brenda will be here for breakfast. Maybe I'll discuss it with her then."

Uncle Bill responded, "I think you both deserve a fair sized wedding to share the happiness with your friends and folks. That's not for me to decide though."

Pete nodded his head solemnly adding, "It's hard to say with her mom and dad in Hawaii. They won't be back for at least another week. At the latest, two weeks from today."

Bill let out another sharp whistle. "Lord Son! Two weeks doesn't give you a whole lot of time."

Pete reminded him, "Let's see what she has to say at breakfast."

After the milking was finished the cows were turned out to pasture. The two men returned to the house for breakfast.

* * *

Brenda greeted Pete at the door with a kiss and then everyone seated themselves around the table. After the blessing was offered they ate with much joy.

As everyone enjoyed cups of coffee and the dishes were cleared Brenda said to Pete, "Honey, I hate to sound pushy, but we should talk about setting a date for our wedding. I don't know how you feel about this but it's my hope that we leave out as husband and wife."

Pete expressed his total agreement and then asked, "When do you expect your mom and dad home?"

Brenda answered, "Not until a week from this Tuesday."

"Let's see now," said Pete, "Do you think we could pull something together for, say, two weeks from today?"

Brenda put her hand on Pete's, "I'm sure we can work something out."

Pete replied, "I'd better call Rob. We should let him know so he doesn't worry about a truck for you. I'm gonna go back to the house and tend to the calves. Brenda, your grandfather should be the first told."

Brenda agreed. "I'll go see him right away."

As Pete was leaving, Brenda panicked, "How am I ever going to get a dress in such a short time?"

Aunt Mae wrapped her arms around the young woman. "Something old, something new, something borrowed, something blue. Child, stand up."

Brenda stood obediently.

"Turn around please."

She obliged.

"Well now, I might need to take it in a bit, but I do believe we have a winner. Come with me Dear."

Brenda slowly followed Aunt Mae up the steps. "You may not like this dress but it will be a very close fit. If you don't like it we'll have to put our heads together, do some cutting, and maybe rub some elbows to come up with your own."

* * *

As Aunt Mae and Brenda entered her sewing room, the aging woman stopped momentarily and gave Brenda another hug.

Without saying another word, she opened the double door closet, took out a long flat box, and sat it down on her worktable.

Brenda was still too overwhelmed to speak.

Small droplets of tears streaked down Mae Dobsin's face as she withdrew the dress from the box. She quickly wiped her face using her sleeve and hung a beautiful wedding gown on the hook stand for Brenda to inspect.

Brenda looked at the dress and began to cry. "Aunt Mae, it's beautiful! I've never seen one like it. It's remarkable. Was it yours?"

She replied, "No, but I know this dress well. Every stitch was done with my own hands. Now if you like it, Dear, try it on."

Brenda quickly donned the dress.

Aunt Mae opened another box and pulled out a long bridal veil.

As Brenda looked at her reflection in the mirror she began to cry again.

At this point, both women were crying joyfully.

Aunt Mae sniffed and again mopped her face. "Turn around Dear. It looks like a perfect fit. It's not too tight around the chest is it? Can you breathe all right?"

Brenda was still too emotional to speak so she simply nodded her head.

"Well Dear, what do you think? Do you want this dress?"

There was a long pause while Brenda pulled herself together. "Yes. It's the most perfect dress I've ever seen."

The aging woman choked, "Well then, we'd better get it to the cleaners. I don't know about you Dear, but I need another cup of coffee...a strong one."

The two women went downstairs and sat at the table recovering over a cup of coffee.

When Brenda had fully regained her composure she asked, "Aunt Mae, who was the dress made for?"

Mae Dobsin took a long sip of her steaming brew then answered, "I hand made that dress for Vicki when she and Pete, Sr. got married. She had hoped one day to pass it on to her own daughter, but she and Pete only had one child. About six months before their accident Vicki gave me the dress for safekeeping. She told me, "Even if little Brenda marries some one other than our Pete, I want her to have my dress." So, Dear, this has been your dress for a long time. Maybe I should have given it to you sooner, but part of me always wanted you and Pete to get together. Another part of me wanted to hold onto the dress for as long as I could."

Both women seemed to develop downspouts around the eyes again.

"Now that's one less worry for you." She scowled over her coffee. "The husband is not supposed to see you in the dress or hear of it until he sees you for the very first time at the wedding. I have some errands to run in town so I'll take the dress in to the cleaners while you go see your grandfather. It looks like we'll have to put off the trip to the cemetery for a couple of days. We have a lot of work to do."

Brenda sat across the table from her grandfather and said, "Grandpa, I have something I want to tell you. It's very important."

"What's on your mind?" he asked. "You have my full attention Kitten."

"Well Grandpa," she said putting her hand on his withered one, "Pete Dobsin asked me to marry him last night."

The old man snorted, "It's about darn time! What took him so long? What did you say?"

Brenda was astonished by his reaction. "I said yes of course."

The old man laughed, "Kitten, that pup has had a crush on you since you were knee high to a heifer. Why, he was so hooked on you he never dated anyone else. Oh well, at least you know a good catch when you see one."

The old man became somber and asked, "Does Tom know yet?"

Brenda shook her head. "Not yet. You're the first I've told."

"Tommy and I had some troubles between us. I'll tell you it was my doin'. His two older sisters married off and moved away. I guess I always had it in my head that Tom would always be here. I never figured he had his own dreams. When he took to driving trucks, let's just say your grandpa was harsh on your daddy. I guess I'm just a stubborn old goat. My pride wouldn't let me tell him how proud I was of him. I just don't know how to apologize."

Brenda witnessed the single tear that rolled down his face.

The weathered man cleared his throat and muttered, "You can't turn back the calendar. Go on now. You're gonna be one busy woman. Remind me Monday. I guess I need to take my suit to the cleaners."

Brenda gave him a hug and a kiss.

* * *

Pete had finished tending to the calves and had taken a long pull of tea. He thought, "I'd better call Rob." He quickly dialed the number on his cell phone.

Millie Wendover answered the phone. "Wendover Trucking, how may I help you?"

Pete responded, "Millie, this is Pete. Is Rob in?"

Millie let out a sigh, "Sure Pete, I'll connect you right away."

"This is Rob. What can I do for you?"

"Rob, it's Pete. Uh, can we talk?"

Rob replied, "Please don't tell me you're having second thoughts. Something has gotta go right today."

Pete quickly responded, "It's not that Rob. I just needed to tell you not to worry about getting Brenda a new truck. You won't need it."

Rob yelled, "Please don't tell me she quit!"

Pete reassured him, "She didn't quit Rob. You won't be needing a truck for her because she and I are getting married. My truck, however, won't be able to roll for about two weeks."

There was a long silence. "I want both of you in my office at 2 o'clock sharp!"

The line went dead.

Pete hurried in to the house to find Brenda. She was tidying up in the kitchen. "Honey, Rob wants to see us in his office at 2 o'clock this afternoon. He sounded kind of strange. I've never heard him this way before."

"It's already 11:30. I guess we'd better hurry then."

Traffic around Indianapolis was slightly heavy due to construction, but they were dutifully in Rob's office right on time.

Rob Wendover didn't say anything. He motioned them into chairs.

The young couple was seated and nervously held hands.

On impulse, their boss rose from his chair and crossed the room to close the door. He sat back down in his chair and was silent for a moment. With a snort of laughter he clasped his hands together and asked, "Why am I always the last to know this stuff? Will someone please tell me what is going on?"

Brenda smiled at him and replied, "Pete and I are getting married and feel it best that we get married before we leave out on the road together."

Pete smiled and nodded his head.

Rob replied, "As your boss I should tell you how much I need that truck rolling." He smiled and added, "As your cousin, Brenda, and as your friend, Pete, I'm going to tell you how happy I am for both of you. What is the timeline? What can we do to help?"

Pete answered, "Two weeks from today. We don't want to get

married without Tom and Phyllis here. We can't take too long off either."

Rob nodded his head. He inquired, "What have you got?"

Brenda chipped in, "A date and a dress."

"Let's see," said Rob. "You'll need a place. Preacher or Justice of the Peace?"

Pete and Brenda looked at each other and agreed they both proffered a minister.

Mr. Wendover nodded his head again. He rose from his chair and firmly placed his knuckles on the windowsill. He was silent for a very long time. He gazed out over the truck yard and noticed his yardman coming out of the new trailer shop. He turned and faced the two with a Cheshire cat grin. "Mind if I stick my nose in and help a little? I can provide place, provisions, and maybe even a minister, all at no cost to you."

Pete and Brenda looked at each other. This time Pete spoke. "Rob, that's too much to ask of you. We can't impose that much."

Rob laughed long and hard for the first time in a week. "Brenda, you're not just my cousin, you're the best company driver I've got, at least you were. Pete, I've asked things of you that I probably wouldn't have done myself. You've always come through for me. Now you two have a near to impossible load to handle. I won't take no for an answer. It's a done deal. Millie and I are stuck with fifty cases of T-bone steaks, and as of today, a full pallet of mixed soft drinks. Quite honestly, that salvage trailer is full. We need to empty it. We've been talking about a safety meeting followed by a cookout. We wanted to wait until Tom and Phyllis got back for a retirement party as well. Why not a wedding too? The new trailer shed will be finished in three days, a full month ahead of schedule. We can hold everything out there. Let's see now, we have the place and the provisions. Now all we need is…" He turned his head toward the yard, "Ah yes, a minister. Wendover Trucking will get one. This will be a big tax write-off." Rob turned and watched as his yardman left the shop to take pump readings. He now had a dangerous grin on his face. He picked up his phone and pushed the intercom button. All over the yard, everyone heard, "Will the Reverend James Jenson please report to my office ASAP?" Rob casually walked over to the door, opened it, and then sat back down.

Within minutes a tall, ebony-skinned man with the disposition of chiseled granite stepped in through the doorway. "This better be good," he growled. "I make it a personal point of conduct not to allow either occupation to interrupt the other."

Rob smiled with ease and replied, "If I would have needed a yard man, I would have called for one. Right now, we need a minister." Rob glanced at Pete and Brenda with a pause, "Say, someone to perform a wedding? Anyone like that here? Have I mistakenly called the wrong man?"

Jim glanced at Pete and Brenda with astonishment. "You mean you two?" Without being invited, Jim walked over to the coffee pot and poured himself a cup. He casually wandered over to the corner of the desk, appearing to ignore the big fuss. He looked the couple over. "Normally, I like to council the couple for at least a month, to make sure they know what they're doing and make sure that they are right for each other. Knowing the both of you for as long as I have, however, I can only say, what the heck took you so long? Never mind. I don't want to know. Praises be sung to high places. I am honored to be asked to join you together. When is this blessed event?"

Pete replied, "Two weeks from today. Is that open for you, Jim?"

Jim slightly grunted, "The first Saturday I have planned off to go fishing. I would gladly put off my poles and cast out my nets to do the work I was called to do for my Master."

"Okay Jim, you can turn down the wind a bit."

"You said yourself Rob, you didn't call for the yard man. You called for the minister."

Everyone laughed.

Jim asked, "Just how are you going to pull this off?"

"Let me get Millie and Vonell in here. I'm going to need their help, too," replied Rob. He picked up the phone and called his wife. "Honey, will you and Vonell please come to my office for a closed-door meeting?"

A few minutes later, the two women arrived and closed the door.

Vonell was the first to speak, "All right Dear, what's going on? I'm smelling something here, and it's real strong. A closed-door meeting, two drivers, the yard man, and now us?"

Brenda was the first to reply. "Pete and I are getting married."

The expression on both women's faces was priceless.

Rob spoke up next. "We have two weeks to put together a wedding without informing anyone in the company, but making sure as many drivers as possible will be in. Millie, I need you to call the rental company and the caterers. Do you know if your brother is available?"

Millie smiled, "I know where this is going. I've got you covered, Hon."

"Vonell, you already know what I need in part."

She gruffly replied, "Yeah, you need me to do a month's amount of work in less than two weeks."

"Well, there's more. I'm sure Pete and Brenda have some friends and family out of state."

Vonell placed her hands on her hips and let out a long sigh. "And we have phones and plenty of people to call, right?"

Rob solemnly nodded.

Vonell gently looked at Pete and Brenda, then warmly smiled. "You know, I can't think of a time any of us asked you for a favor that you have not come through for us, even in the most impossible of circumstances. You better believe I'll do this. I will need a list of names and phone numbers by noon Monday. You got a fax machine available out there?"

Pete nodded. "We have one. We'll call as many people we can on that list first."

Vonell said, "Okay. Make sure you mark off on the list the ones that are confirmed. Find out if they'll need a room. The motel will want at least two weeks notice so the rooms will be available."

Rob agreed, "I forgot about that."

Vonell snapped, "Aren't you glad someone's on their toes here?"

Everyone laughed.

Rob asked, "Hey Jimmy, what kind of food goodies do we have out there in the salvage wagon?'

James replied, "You'll have to talk to the yard man. You called for the minister."

The entire office erupted with hearty laughter.

"I'll have a list for you by 4 o'clock. We just had more stuff come in."

Millie added, "I hate to break up the party but what about bridesmaids, best man…? People need to wear clothing."

Rob agreed. "I'll need to get a hold of your best man and find out what he's wearing. Brenda, you need to get a hold of your bridesmaid, and she'll need a dress. Pete, who are you going to have for your best man? He'll need to know what he's going to wear if he takes the job. Do you have someone in mind?"

Pete answered, "I do. As a matter of fact he works here."

"Well, when you ask him, make sure you tell him I'll fire him if he doesn't say yes," Rob laughed.

Pete smiled, "Rob, will you be the best man at my wedding?"

Rob stared at his friend for a long moment. "You got it my friend. Besides, it'd be kind of hard to fire myself."

Millie asked Brenda, "Who do you have in mind for your maid of honor?"

She answered, "I'd like to ask LeyAnn."

Jim interrupted, "Our LeyAnn, our daughter-in-law?"

Brenda nodded her head. "Do you know if she's at home right now?"

Rob responded, "If you want to talk to her, just head over to the warehouse. She's running it now. I hired her last week."

Jim smiled. "Broadus will be proud of her."

Brenda stood and said, "If you'll excuse me for a few minutes, I need to go see LeyAnn." Brenda left the office and crossed the yard to the warehouse.

* * *

"LeyAnn?" she called. "May I have a minute of your time?"

The girl on the forklift replied, "Give me a minute, I have a few pallets I need to restack. Is it important?"

Brenda nodded her head smiling.

"Well, what is it?"

Brenda replied, "I'd like to take you shopping with me this afternoon."

LeyAnn quickly pulled the forklift to a halt and stepped off. "What's so important about going shopping? We can do that any time. What's so important that you need to buy it now? I'm kind of busy."

Brenda answered, "I need to buy you a new dress."

LeyAnn put her hands on her hips and stomped her left foot. "What makes you think I want to wear a dress? What's the occasion?"

Brenda softly replied, "Pete and I are getting married two weeks from today. I want you to be my maid of honor. That's why you need the dress."

Amidst her shock, she stammered, "I…I'll get off at 4 o'clock. Yes!"

The two women embraced.

"You and Pete?"

Brenda nodded. "He asked me last night."

LeyAnn asked, "Do you need a dress?"

Brenda answered, "I got it."

LeyAnn asked in wonder, "Pete asked you last night and you've already got a dress?"

Brenda nodded again. "I'll fill you in while we're shopping. Do you have wheels? Pete and I spent the day together and my truck is at his house."

LeyAnn smiled, "So you need me to take you out to his place?"

Brenda said, "I'll need to find out what the guys are up to. Pete and his best man need to find out what they'll need to wear to match. I'll let you know at 4 o'clock."

As Brenda left the warehouse she laughed as LeyAnn let out a loud yell. "Yeah!" she cried.

* * *

Brenda was back in Rob's office and gave everyone a thumb's up. "I have my maid of honor. We're gonna go shopping after she gets off work."

Rob looked at his wife, "Millie, why don't you take the company car. Get the girls and take them wherever they need to go. Pete and I will take our car." He added with a grim look, "We'll get sized up for the tuxes. Vonell, is Broadus back from the road yet?"

She smiled, "He just pulled into the yard."

Rob replied, "I'll catch him. Since his wife will be tied up he can hang with us. Then we'll all go out to dinner."

Pete said, "It sounds like a plan. Dinner is on me."

Rob added, "Jim, why don't you call Rose and ask her to meet us. We'll all meet at the Chinese Buffet, say at 8 o'clock."

As everyone was leaving they met Broadus in the driver's lounge. "Sure I'll join you, but let me get a shower first," he said.

* * *

As 8 o'clock approached, everyone was relieved to have had a successful shopping trip. Brenda would only discuss her dress with Millie, and with help from Millie and a prominent mall store employee, they found LeyAnn a perfect dress. Brenda also decided she really wanted Millie in the wedding party. She felt it important to call Pete immediately on the cell phone.

He readily agreed.

They decided that Pete should add one more person as well. He closed the conversation with Brenda, "Honey, I've been thinking about that myself and I've already got the guy in mind. I love you. I'll talk to you later."

As the salesman was finishing up with Rob, Pete laughed and said, "Two down, one to go."

Broadus answered, "I sure feel sorry for whoever that third sucker is."

Rob caught on instantly. Both men grinned wickedly. "Suit him up!"

"Awe, no," groaned Broadus.

"No way!" Rob chuckled. "Son, think of it this way, if I've gotta hold a shot gun to his back, someone's gotta hold the ammo."

Pete replied, "Broadus, if you really don't want to, I can't make you."

Broadus said, "Pete, it's not that I don't want to. Things are a bit tight for us. I want to, but I can't afford it. Right now $75 is a lot of money."

Rob answered immediately, "I'm picking up the tab."

Pete looked at Rob, "No, I'm doing this. You're already doing too much."

Broadus looked long and hard at his friend Pete. "When Rob didn't have any trainers available, you took me out. You trained me. When Dad and I had our disagreements, you let me air them without interfering. When LeyAnn and I got married and the transmission in our car went out, you rented us a car so we wouldn't have to miss our honeymoon." He closed his eyes and let out a sigh. "Pete, I would be honored to be in your wedding."

Later that night, with everyone sitting around the dinner table, spirits were high.

Bright and early the next morning, Pete faithfully arrived at the milk house for the milking. Again, every time the two men would speak, the cows would listen in.

Uncle Bill asked, "So you got your party all together yet?"

Pete said, "Yes. Rob's got the shotgun and Broadus will carry the ammo. LeyAnn is maid of honor. Millie is the bridesmaid."

Uncle Bill chuckled, "You oughta have Calli as the flower girl and Clutch as the ring bearer."

Suddenly Pete was silent. "Uncle Bill, I think you're on to something. After all, we're all going to be one happy family."

Uncle Bill smiled, "I was only kidding, Son, cracking a joke. Not like you can fit a tux on a kitten or a dress on that calico."

"It will have to be checked into with Brenda of course."

Uncle Bill scratched the bald spot on his head. "How are you gonna talk the kittens into this?"

"Thank you for reminding me Uncle Bill. Brenda and I have been so busy we haven't even told the kittens yet."

Uncle Bill laughed, "Just tell Boots. She can let everyone know at the next farm council."

Pete answered, "Brenda and I have been neglecting the kittens. That's wrong."

At breakfast, Pete and Brenda seriously discussed having Clutch and Calli in the wedding party.

"Anyway," Brenda said, "we better get back to the house and ready for services. "I promised I'd pick up my grandfather on the way."

Aunt Mae dropped her fork. "What did you do or say to get your grandfather to come back to the congregation?"

Brenda smiled, "I just told him that since my father was not yet available, I needed him, the eldest living of the Kingmans, to publicly announce our wedding at the church."

"Didn't he put up a fight?" inquired Aunt Mae.

Brenda responded, "He said he couldn't because he didn't have a suit to wear for that kind of occasion, so I took him out and bought him one."

"You always did have old Tom wrapped around your finger," stated Uncle Bill.

Everyone laughed.

Aunt Mae nodded. "You always have had a special way with your grandpa. Maybe it's not such a bad thing."

At the small county chapel, the Kingman-Dobsin family filled and entire pew. Much attention was drawn by the eldest Kingman.

Once the morning service was over, but before the congregation was dismissed, the minister asked if anyone wished to make any announcements."

Thomas Kingman, Sr. stood. After a reflection of fifty-six years of faithful service, he had now been absent for almost 5 years. He cleared his throat and looked at the minister, the same man who presided over his Emily's funeral, and spoke. "I've come here today to announce the engagement and upcoming wedding of my only grandchild, Brenda Kingman, to Peter Dobsin, Jr. And let me add, it's about darn time."

The minister led the congregation in a short prayer of thanks and a blessing upon the upcoming wedding. He then asked the young couple to stand. "So Peter, Brenda, tell us how this came about."

Pete said, "Friday evening I asked Brenda to be my wife. Believe it or not, the arrangements are already set. The wedding will take place on the grounds of Wendover Trucking at 1 o'clock on the tenth. It is our privilege and pleasure to welcome this congregation to celebrate with us. There will be plenty of food and entertainment. If you plan to attend, we need to be informed by this Friday so we can provide ample seating."

The minister let the congregation in a round of applause and a prayer of thanks. With no other announcements, the service was dismissed.

Outside, everyone gathered around Pete and Brenda to shake their hands and congratulate them.

Aunt Mae asked Tom Kingman, Sr. to enjoy a lunch at their home, an invitation he hesitantly accepted.

After a pleasurable lunch, Mr. Kingman volunteered to take a head count of the calves as they were loaded onto the trucks.

Brenda and Aunt Mae filled syringes for Pete and Uncle Bill while they administered them to the calves that were marked for sale.

The entire job was completed by 4:30.

Brenda's grandfather casually asked Pete, "About how much do you think you'll make on this lot?"

Pete smiled at the aging man, "At current market price, I should make $63,000 after expenses."

Mr. Kingman wiped his forehead and said, "Wow! I can remember when you were lucky to get $30 for a calf."

Pete nodded, "Yes, Sir, but these calves are going to international market. They are going to be used as breeders."

"Now, out of curiosity," inquired Mr. Kingman, "what do those shots cost?"

Pete laughed, "Each calf got a $75 gift in its rump."

Both men chuckled.

* * *

Brenda's grandfather was a little tired so she drove him home.

She and Pete were determined to spend the rest of the day with Clutch and Calli. They strolled hand in hand around the farm looking for their kittens. After a few minutes they were located napping in the shade of the tractor shed. Although they hated to wake them, they really were quite anxious to spend time with them.

Pete carried a blanket over his right shoulder, which he spread under a sprawling apple tree next to one of the ponds.

After several minutes of playing with the kittens, Pete finally spoke up. "Calli, Clutch, Brenda and I have something we want you to know. Plans have changed a little. We're not to leave out for about two weeks. I have asked Brenda to be my wife and she's agreed."

Both kittens looked at them with interest as if they actually understood what the humans were saying.

Brenda spoke next. "Calli, what this means is, when we leave out on the road, we are all going to be one big happy family."

Pete reached out his hand and scratched Calli's ears. "Little one, this is going to be your new home. Understand, we will all still leave out together when it's time to go back to work. We just won't be alone for long periods of time."

Brenda added, "That is, of course, unless one of us girls gets pregnant."

Pete spoke again, "We are going to do our best to make sure you two are in the wedding. I just hope you two understand what this means."

The rest of the afternoon was spent with the four of them in play.

Clutch tried to get Calli to join him in chasing minnows around the pond's edge. Her last experience around that much water caused her to feel wary.

Clutch asked, "Why don't you want to chase the fish?"

Calli replied, "Are you sure there's not any monsters in there?"

Clutch answered, "There are things called turtles, but they'll leave you alone. I don't think they'll hurt you anyway. They're real easy to spot. They kind of look like smooth, round rocks with four legs, a head, and a tail. Mother says it's okay to play with the smaller ones. We shouldn't bother the large ones, and we shouldn't be cruel to any of them. Even they have work to do on the farm. She says they keep the ponds clean."

Just then a frog jumped into the pond in front of the kittens. Calli rushed to hide behind Clutch and yelled, "A jumping monster!"

Clutch reassured her, "It's okay, it's only a frog. They won't bite you. They eat bugs. Besides, they're fun to chase."

Suddenly Calli was distracted by something with Clutch. "Clutch, you're getting spots! Are you sick?"

He replied, "I don't think so. I feel great. How many are there?"

She answered, "I don't know. I can't count. Are you sure you're not sick?"

Clutch said, "I'm fine. Mother told me I might get more as I grow older. I'm sure it's no big deal."

Pete and Brenda sat together on the blanket. Then she asked, "Do you think they understood what we told them?"

Pete replied, "I think they understand us, but they can't respond in a way we understand. I believe the kittens knew that something big was coming up and that it's a good thing."

Brenda answered, "I've always believed that for myself. Pete, do you think you'll ever get out of trucking? We've gotta start thinking about the future."

Pete looked deeply into her eyes. "Honey, if we ever have children, we'll need to be full-time parents. Uncle Bill is starting to get some age to him. Sooner or later I'm going to have to assume the full responsibilities of the family farm. It will never do to see one inch of Dobsin land leave the family. This land has been in the family since Indiana was homesteaded. I can't let it end with me. How do you feel Brenda? You're the best trucker I've ever known. It's in your blood."

She smiled and replied, "Every path has a beginning and an end. Sure, I've followed in Dad's path. Mom was jealous of that. What she doesn't know is how much I wish I could be like her. Don't get me wrong Pete, I love what I do. But what I wouldn't give to be like my mother."

Pete kissed her hand and asked, "So you would settle for being a farmer's wife when the time comes?"

Brenda lightly tapped him on the nose. "Bad puppy, it was the farm boy I fell in love with when I was 8 years old. We don't wanna wind up like my dad. Don't get me wrong. I love him dearly, but only now, after all these years, has he just rediscovered his own wife."

Pete solemnly nodded his head. "I can understand. I lost both of my parents to that kind of living. I guess we'd better get the kittens back. It's getting late."

Brenda replied, "Yeah, we should get them back to the other cats while we still can. Pete, have you noticed anything different about Clutch?"

Pete took a long look at his kitten. "Wow! He's picking up spots! It's cute isn't it? He is part bob. Either way, he's ours."

Before the sun had completely dropped beyond the western sky, the kittens were returned to where they had been napping. All of the other animals were lounging around as though nothing was happening.

As soon as Pete and Brenda were out of sight and hearing distance, Scrappy yapped, "Okay, okay, what did they say? Tell us!"

Drowser barked out, "Hold on, Pup. Tabby, shall I call council now?"

She meowed, "Absolutely Drowser."

Drowser sounded the call for council. All of the animals headed for the meadow.

All of the animals were talking at once.

Boots let out a long 'moo' to call the animals to order. When everyone was silent Boots thanked them all for coming. She moved on, "It seems we have a number of conflicting reports. Rita, will you please tell everyone what you overheard in the milk barn?"

She responded with, "I think Mr. Dobsin is going to get shot and doesn't mind! Either that or they're going hunting. He said his friend Rob was gonna hold a shotgun to his back and his friend Broadus was bringing the ammunition."

Boots called upon Scrappy next. "Tell us what you overheard."

Scrappy barked out, "I was listening in on Aunt Mae Dobsin when she was talking on the rock and vine, uh, I mean the phone. I think Pete and Brenda are only going swimming because Aunt Mae Dobsin said, 'I believe he's finally taking the plunge,' and 'Of all the fish in the sea, he got the perfect catch.'"

Several of the others were called upon to give a report.

Finally, Boots demanded of Tabby, "Do your kittens have any words for us?"

She smiled and looked to the rest of the council. "The kittens have spent the entire afternoon with their humans. Kids, if it's not too private, please share with the farm council what you heard today."

There was a bit of noise as the council was joined by one last animal.

Boots mooed an acknowledgement to the latecomer.

As he took a place in the council circle he nodded respectfully. It was the Great Tomcat of the Woods. No one would dare question him. He belonged.

Clutch was absolutely speechless in his presence.

"Kittens," he called, "I believe you were about to share some information with this council. Please continue."

Clutch and Calli took turns sharing the information that was given to them by Pete and Brenda. It was very clear to everyone that Pete Dobsin was not going to get shot. All of the council members agreed that what was going to happen was the best thing they had heard on the farm in a very long time.

Closing comments were given by the Great Cat himself. "Many

tragedies have been known to this farm and family. I say this to you now—Love is the strength that makes all good things happen here."

As soon as the council was dismissed by Boots, the Great Cat disappeared.

Clutch strained hard to see where the Great Cat had gone, but he was unable. He had many questions he wanted to ask, yet was unsure who to talk to.

That evening Clutch's mother approached Calli. She asked, "Would you like to mouse with me tonight?"

Calli looked at her with much admiration but dropped her head. "I don't know how." She would not look at her. She was too ashamed.

Tabby smiled, "You should always look at the one you are talking to." On a lighter note she said, "None of us are born knowing how to mouse. I wasn't. It's a skill we develop. My mother taught me, just as her mother taught her."

Once again Calli felt a familiar pain. "I don't have a mother to teach me. She's dead."

"I see," said Tabby. "Being a mother goes far beyond giving birth. What would you say dear, if I told you that Della and I are sisters?"

Calli looked at her strangely. "Miss Tabby, isn't Della a dog?"

Tabby laughed. "Indeed she is, and a rather big one, isn't she? Her mother's name was Margie. Margie had four puppies. Della is the only one that lived. Margie died two days after Della was born. My mother had too much milk. Only two of her kittens had survived. A strange tomcat killed the rest. My mother nursed Della.

Of course my mother knew Della was a puppy. Della had a lot of trouble trying to learn how to mouse. Drowser helped and look at what a fine dog she has become. To my mother, Della was still her daughter. I will never ask you, Child, to forget your mother, but I can certainly teach you how to mouse if you'd like to learn. Quite personally I think you have the makings to be a great mouser."

Calli asked, "Can I be as good as you?"

Tabby smiled, "Perhaps better."

As Tabby and Calli made their way to the barn, Tabby explained some of the basics. "Even the way kittens play is training for mousing." Tabby also explained some of the ways of catching mice.

When they reached the barn, Calli inquired, "Miss Tabby, what do we do with them after we've caught them?"

Tabby looked at her and softly said, "We kill them Dear."

"Dead?" Calli asked.

Tabby replied, "Quite dead, Calli."

"Miss Tabby, why do we have to kill them? Isn't that harsh?"

Tabby said, "Sit down Dear. I will explain. One female mouse may have twelve or more babies at a time. Let's see, I would say you are about three months old and are growing well. A mouse has about two months before those babies will mature to where they are ready to breed themselves. You will not be mature enough to breed until you about ten or eleven months old. If one mouse has twelve babies every three months, that one can become over 100 before you know it. Calli, don't think of what we do as cruel. Mice carry diseases. They eat their way into the grain bags and leave their waste everywhere they go. If their waste gets into the food supply, animals and humans alike can become ill and die. If they leave their waste in the cows' food, it can even poison their milk. I have even heard stories where large populations of humans died because the grain they ate was poisoned by mice. Please don't think I'm prejudiced. It is our duty to kill mice. Many animals feed off of mice, even poisonous snakes. Say a copperhead comes into the barn to hunt mice and Bill or Pete doesn't see it. That snake might bite them. They can die. That same snake might bite a cow. Then she dies too. I know for a fact that if someone from the milk factory inspects the barn and sees mouse waste they will refuse to buy the milk. The farm would shut down in a week because we didn't do our job."

Calli mewed, "I think I understand. Mice are very dirty, and by killing them we help to keep the farm clean." Calli dropped her head again. She looked up at Tabby and asked, "Will Clutch be proud of me if I do a good job?"

Tabby gave a smile, as only a cat can. "Just between you and me Girl, he already is."

Calli meowed. "What if I don't do a good job?"

Tabby chuckled, "You will do fine. It is only your first night. Sometimes it takes time to catch on to it all." Tabby looked around to make sure no one else was close enough to hear. She whispered to Calli, "I didn't catch one until my fifth night. Promise not to tell?"

Calli let out a growl. "I won't tell! I'm ready! Miss Tabby, what do we do with them after we kill them? Do we eat them?"

Tabby answered, "I always put mine along the wall to the tank room. Mr. Bill counts them and then disposes of them. If we're still in the barn when he comes in to work, we get a pat on the head and milk out of the first full strip cup. All of the others wait."

* * *

The next morning, when Pete and Uncle Bill came into the milk barn, the two cats sat proudly beside their night's kill. Calli had killed three mice.

"Tabby!" proclaimed Uncle Bill, "It looks like you've got a first rate student with ya'! Pete, why don't you wash and strip your first pour so these hard workin' girls can have a treat."

Pete reached down and scratched Calli's ears. "Calli, with work like this, Tabby might put up a fight when it comes time for us to go back on the road."

Calli didn't like what he had to say, but she purred anyway.

When the two cats left the barn they were not displeased to announce that Calli had killed three mice in her first night.

Even Della raised her ears on that. She was so impressed with Calli's skills that she pointed her nose to the sky and barked, "You did good, Kid," and trotted away.

By noon Monday Pete and Brenda had faxed their list of names and phone numbers to Vonell. They kept a select list to call themselves. They had also promised Vonell a list of their friends in their hometown by Friday. She was to inform all guests to dress casually.

At about 5 p.m. Brenda's cell phone rang.

"Daddy!" she exclaimed. "I'm glad you called! We need to talk."

"Calm down Sugar. Tell my neighbor I'll cut the grass when I get home."

"Dad," Brenda chided. "Is Mom there?"

"Nah, she's in the market place right now probably haggling prices over a dress or something."

"Daddy, while you're in Hawaii why don't you go shopping with Mom? Maybe you could buy yourself a suit."

"Sugar, that's not funny. The only way you will ever see me in a suit is when you get married."

Brenda asked, "Daddy, when are you and Mom coming home?"

He replied, "We come back to Indy Wednesday of next week. Why do you feel I need a suit?"

Brenda answered, "For my wedding, of course! Pete and I are getting married three days after you come home!"

There was a long silence. "I must be having a problem with my cell phone, distance and all. It sounded like you said that you and Pete are getting married. Was that just static?"

"No Daddy. That's what I said. Friday he asked me to be his wife. I said yes. We don't want to drive team together unless we are married."

Tom sniffed a couple of times. "Darned salt air, it's messing with my sinuses. Don't you think this is kind of sudden?"

Brenda laughed. "Sudden? I've had a crush on Pete for years! You know that! Not to mention the fact that you've been playing match maker for a long time."

"Sugar, I don't know what to say. I really do want you two together. I just didn't think it would be so soon. I'm sorry. I'm really happy for the both of you. It's wonderful! I've been wanting to hear you say this for a long time. It just caught me off guard. I love it! Have you told your grandfather yet?"

"Yes Daddy."

"How does he feel about it?"

"Grandpa thinks it's wonderful!"

"Well, I don't know how I'm going to tell your mother, but I'll figure it out."

She said, "Thank you Daddy."

"Sugar, are you sure this is what you want?"

Brenda replied, "I've waited a long time to tell you this. Yes!"

He said, "You most certainly have our blessing. I gotta know. How in the blazes were you two able to arrange a wedding fit for a Kingman in only two weeks?"

"I don't have time to fill you in on the details now. We'll tell you everything as soon as you get home."

"Brenda, I don't know how I'm going to tell your mother yet, but I'll let her know. I love you!"

Brenda replied, "I love you too."

As Phyllis approached her husband, he sat gazing out at the waves holding a glass of iced tea.

"You better be staring at the waves and not the swimsuits, Husband."

He replied, "Sorry Dear. Although the scenery may be appealing, I was just sitting here thinking."

Phyllis shot back, "Don't tell me you're already missing the smell of diesel."

He inquired, "Well anyway Dear, how was shopping?"

She triumphantly held out a package. "That man in the market place was asking $50, but I got him down to $25."

Tom mused, "Well, Dear, maybe we can go tomorrow and see if you can get me a suit for $25."

His wife snorted, "Ha! You go shopping with me? You won't even go with me to the grocery store! You wait in the car. What is all this nonsense about suits? You hate them. You want to go shopping with me? For a suit? Riiight. How many times have you said, 'The only way I'll put on a suit is if Brenda gets ma…' Thomas Edward Kingman, Jr.! What's going on?"

Tom continued to muse, "Oh, nothing much, just Pete and Brenda getting married."

His lovely wife dropped her dress in the sand. She shouted, "What did you say?"

Tom took a long pull of his iced tea. "I said Pete and Brenda are getting married. Dear, I think your dress is getting dirty."

She demanded, "How? When? Oh, whatever! Fill me in now! How did you find out?"

He calmly replied, "While you were shopping I called Brenda. Apparently Friday evening Pete Dobsin, Jr. asked our Brenda to marry him." He stood up and gave his wife a hug and a kiss. "It seems that all of the arrangements have already been made. Robby has got to have his hands in this."

When Phyllis finally regained her composure she took a deep breath and asked, "When is the wedding? There's going to be a lot of things to do."

He answered, "We have plenty of time. It's three days after we get back home."

Phyllis erupted, "Three days? We only have three days after we get home? Our daughter is only giving us three days?"

People standing within earshot began to clap and cheer their congratulations.

Tom laughed. "Yup. Three days. It's plenty of time."

She continued to panic. "But I have to get my dress to the cleaners!"

Tom reassured her, "Brenda's already taken care of it. Look, I don't know all of the arrangements, but I'll find out." Tom bent down and picked up his wife's dress and smiled, "Why don't we go back to the market place and get me some shorts and a shirt to match this dress?" He put his iced tea down on the tray and waited casually for his wife's shock to wear off.

Suddenly Phyllis grabbed him by the arm. "Let's go Too Long. We're getting you a suit NOW!"

Tom dropped a buck on the tray and left with his wife as the crowd of people cheered. Tom added, "We may have a problem finding a place to buy a suit."

Phyllis insisted, "Not so fast dear. They happen to have one in the hotel. You're not getting out of it. They even have a tailor on staff. I did some looking." As they entered the lobby of the hotel Phyllis dragged her husband to the front desk. "Will you please direct us to the men's store? My husband, whether he likes it or not, is getting a new suit."

The man behind the counter motioned for a bellboy. "William, please show Mr. and Mrs. Kingman to our men's shop."

* * *

As they entered the men's store a gentleman appeared and offered his assistance.

Phyllis blurted out, "My daughter needs a suit for my husband's wedding! I mean…"

Tom interrupted, "I need a suit Sir."

The salesman smiled. "Mrs. Kingman, would you like something to drink while you're waiting?"

Tom interjected, "You better bring her something strong, and I'll have something tall, amber, and foaming, please."

As the salesman led Tom to a suit rack he added with a smile, "I take it that this is for your daughter's wedding."

The salesman sent a lady to ask if Phyllis needed a dress.

Phyllis explained to her that she already had a dress and gave a full description of it so her husband's suit would match.

Two hours later the salesman had set Tom up with a navy blue suit, a white dress shirt, and a necktie that was the same color as his wife's dress.

Phyllis asked, "What are you gonna do about shoes?"

Tom smiled, "Just polish up my black boots."

She exclaimed, "Thomas Edward Kingman, Jr.!"

He sighed, chuckling, "I'm just kidding. I picked up black wing tips. Now are you happy?" He looked at the salesman, "How much is this going to cost?" It suddenly dawned on Tom, "Mister, how did you know my name is Kingman?"

The salesman replied, "Sir, a man called from Indianapolis today, only ten minutes before you came in. The description he gave… You are Mr. Kingman aren't you?"

"Yes."

He continued, "The man said to deck you out like a minister and to put it on your hotel bill. He's picking up the tab. The only thing I'm supposed to tell you is, 'Got ya' Uncle Tom.'"

Tom exclaimed, "Phyllis, remind me to bend that boy over my knee."

Tom was informed, "Your suit will be delivered to your room by noon tomorrow. You don't have to be there. I'll also have everything else delivered then too."

Tom dropped a $10 bill on the counter and said, "Here, go buy yourself a handkerchief. And how much for the beverages?"

The man tucked the money into his pocket and replied, "They're on the house. Have a nice day."

Tom kissed his wife and said, "Dear, why don't you go and do some more shopping. I have another call to make. I think I'm going to call Robby."

Phyllis sensed the mood her husband was in and said, "I'm going shopping dear. See you in the room."

* * *

The phone rang at Rob's office. He answered, "Rob Wendover, how can I help you?"

There was a brief pause on the other end. "Rob, this is Tom."

"Hey Uncle Tom. How is Hawaii?"

Rob heard a few sniffs. "Darned salt air. Anyway, I just wanted to call and say thank you. But I still want to turn you over my knee when I get back. How did you know that Phyllis would take me to the men's shop at the hotel?"

Rob answered, "Brenda called me right after she talked to you. She kind of figured Aunt Phyllis would insist on getting you a new suit immediately. I called your hotel to see if they had a tailor shop. The manager agreed to add your expenses to the bill. He patched me through to the store. And just in case Aunt Phyllis did not react that way, I had the store clerk leave a message for you at the front desk. Either way, you were taken care of. I even told him to have a couple of bottles of golden juice. You were going to need it. By the way, your daughter won a $5 bet at your expense. She said Aunt Phyllis would drag you into the men's shop within ten hours. I said you'd drag your feet until tomorrow morning."

"Yeah," said Tom. "Either way I lose."

Both men laughed.

Tom inquired, "How is this all going to fall into place?"

Rob Wendover filled his uncle in on all of the details as had been planned up to that point.

Tom finished by saying, "Let's see if I have this correct. The wedding is hush-hush. The story line is safety meeting, BBQ, and my retirement party, all of it three days after we get back home? That's pretty darned sneaky. Son, I like it! I'll bring Phyllis up to date on everything. I'm still going to turn you over my knee though. You can't stop me or fire me now. Bye now."

Tabby went off to work, this time taking Clutch's brother with
her.

Clutch was unable to sleep. He silently slipped away from the
other kittens over to where Drowser sat looking up at the stars.

Drowser, never looking down at him, asked, "Shouldn't you be
sleeping Son?"

Clutch replied, "I…I couldn't sleep Sir. I just have some things
on my mind, and they're things I don't know if I want to talk to my
mother about or not. There are some question I have that I don't
know who to ask, or even if I should ask them at all."

Drowser asked, "Sorta like guy talk maybe?"

Clutch answered, "I think so, but I'm not sure. Uncle Drowser,
can I talk to you about it? Can we have guy talk?"

The old dog's heart was moved at being called 'Uncle' by this
kitten. "Well," he said, "I'm not going to promise this old dog has
all the answers, but I'll give it a try." The old dog looked at Clutch
with soft eyes and then asked, "So what's eating at your tail Son?"

Clutch wasn't sure how to put his thoughts into words, but he
finally asked, "Why do I look different than my brother and
sisters?"

"Different?" inquired Drowser. "How so?"

He responded, "Well, my brother and I were playing in the soft mud by the pond. When we looked into the water we could see ourselves."

Drowser chuckled a little. "You saw your reflections."

Clutch nodded his head. "Yes Sir. I looked different than my brother. I'm bigger. My head is shaped different, and I'm getting spots all over. They don't wash off either. Some humans have said I look like I'm part bobcat. Even my tail is shorter than my brother's. I have heard stories that sometimes animals will take another animal's baby. I think they call it 'adopting.' Is Miss Tabby really my mother, or did I belong to someone else?"

Drowser laughed lightly and barked, "Son, I think it's time you learn about the cows and the chickens. Listen to Old Drowser and I'll explain things. We'll start out by talking about your Pete and Brenda. You know they're gonna get married. When two humans get married it is a commitment, a promise. The two of them are going to do everything together, including breeding. With that promise, they will only breed with each other. It's not quite like that with animals. Over the course of maybe four or five days a female cat or dog may breed with several males, or just one male several times. It is very possible that one kitten or more may not have the same father. That's not a bad thing Son, at least not for animals. Every kind of animal is different. Here we have about forty-five chickens. Miss Penny is the lead chicken. We have two roosters here. Chickens lay eggs. They're only eggs unless a rooster breeds with the hens. If the rooster breeds with a hen a baby chick will grow inside the shell. Now onto cows. A farmer selects what bull a cow is mated with. That's so a calf can come from a good bloodline. A cow has to have a calf before she can give milk."

Clutch nodded his head.

"You see, Clutch, no two cows look alike. Miss Tabby most certainly is your birth mother. It's okay to look a little different than you litter mates." Drowser looked at Clutch. "What else is caught in your fur?"

"Uncle Drowser, how come I feel funny when I'm around Calli?"

Drowser looked at him long and hard. "What kind of feeling funny is it?"

Clutch answered, "I guess it's a silly question."

Drowser said, "Oh, I don't know. Let's see if we can figure this out."

Clutch responded, "Sometimes when I'm with her it's like it doesn't matter what she says. I just feel good beside her. Even if we disagree on something, I just like being with her. Sometimes, when we're not together, I get a feeling sort of like having a hairball, but I can't get rid of it. When something is hurtful to her I want to take the hurt away and make her feel better."

"Hmmm," said Drowser. "I'm not real certain, but maybe we should hold off on that one for a while. It sounds like the beginning stages of love." He again gave the kitten a considering look. "Tell me, Son, what else is on your mind?"

Clutch answered, "Uncle Drowser, how did the Great Tom Cat become part of our farm?"

Drowser looked at him for a long time, not quite certain he wanted to go in that direction. He was pretty sure where the questions were leading, but he had never believed in telling anything but the truth. "He came a number of years ago, I don't remember how many. It's been a while, maybe as many as ten years now. In the spring Mr. Bill and Miss Mae tend to go on walks. Everything is new. This spring, when them two was taking one of their walks in the woods, they heard a gun go off. As a matter of fact, I was with 'em. They don't allow anybody outside the farm to hunt their land, not to mention, it was not a hunting time of year. Somebody shot a female bobcat. She had a big belly. She wasn't dead, but she was hurt real bad. Mr. Bill talked about putting her out of her pain. But Miss Mae told him, 'Oh no! She's gonna have babies. They deserve every chance they can get.' She was hurt so bad that she couldn't even fight anymore. Mr. Bill carefully wrapped her up in his shirt. That bobcat held onto life for about two weeks. Right there in the kitchen she gave life to three baby kittens. She didn't like being taken care of by humans, but she knew they were trying to help her so she didn't try to bite them. She ate what she could. Three days after those kittens were born she couldn't fight anymore. She died, Son." Drowser sniffed a couple of times. "Life is a precious thing to the Dobsins and to us. Miss Mae worked even harder to take care of those babies. Sometimes nature wins. Two of them didn't make it— not for lack of trying by Miss Mae. It just happens. With the third one, it just so happened that there was a nursing cat here. A strange tomcat had come around and killed a couple. One morning, while Miss Mae was hanging out clothes to dry, Miss Sally, that'd be Miss Tabby's momma, snuck inside the house and stole that little bobcat kitten away. Miss Mae was so frantic over the kitten being missing she called Mr. Bill in from the fields. Then she called to his brother's house, that'd be Pete's mom and dad, for help searching. Them poor humans searched high and low. I was looking too. We covered the whole farm, or so we thought. You know where the old silo used to be, the round patch by the barn?"

Clutch didn't know what a silo was, but he knew the round patch by the barn. He nodded his head.

"The silo is gone now, but there was a small area behind it—real soft grass. All the people were standing by the silo when little Pete, course he ain't so little now, said he heard a kitten noise. He looked back there and, sure enough, there was Miss Sally, giving her milk to her last surviving kitten and the one she swiped. Even though nature can sometimes seem harsh, it can also be good too. Everything has a purpose. All those human folks just smiled. Miss Mae told Mr. Bill, 'Let's take them to the kitchen. We are not losing any more kittens.' When that little guy's eyes first opened it was Miss Sally he saw. It was natural that he saw her as his mother. Miss Sally didn't know much about wild animals so to her, he was her son. For all intents and purposes he saw himself as a farm cat. I even shared a paw in his teaching. He could mouse, and he was real good at it. His sister was good too. He kept getting bigger and bigger, and his mousing skills got better and better. Before long, he was hunting rats and full-grown rabbits. The Dobsins don't keep house animals. If one is sick or hurt, they'll take it in and mend it if it's small enough, but all of us animals are outside. We are the eyes and ears of the farm. I don't know what made him change, but he started to realize that he wasn't an ordinary cat. He started going to the woods, which is off limits to all puppies, kittens, and other small animals. The woods has it's own dangers. I guess he just figured out for himself where he belongs. We know he's always on the watch and he's always a part of us too. Sometimes he takes out animals that are coming here to do harm. He'll still come in to take milk from the pan that Mr. Bill puts out when he's done milking and to get his ears scratched by Aunt Mae. This is his home and always will be. He is faithful to this farm and the humans know it. Mr. Bill and Mr. Pete, Jr. do go hunting. Every year, well, let's just say they never come home empty handed. I wouldn't be surprised if they maybe got a little extra help."

Clutch asked, "My human kills animals?"

Drowser answered, "Yes, but not without good cause. See, certain animals need meat to live. It's part of what's called the food chain. It kind of works like this; the farmer plants the crops, the rabbits come and eat the crops, security on the farm kills the rabbits. It kind of works the same with mice and good mouse cats. Deer eat the plants too. In their season the farmer goes into the woods and takes a couple of flannel deer. The deer only need a couple of males to breed the females. Mr. Bill and Mr. Pete, Jr. only take enough to eat on. I have seen with my own eyes, both of them finding an orphaned fawn and caring for it until it can take care of itself. Then they turn it loose. There are many kinds of killing. No animal has been killed without reason on this farm. Let's look at the cows. The cows on Mr. Pete's land are all raised for food purposes. About six months ago one of Mr. Bill's milk cows had a bad fall and broke her hip. She was in a lot of pain. He could not fix what was broken because of her size. Mr. Bill had to put her down. It was the kind thing to do, the right thing. To tell you the truth Son, it hurt him real bad to have to do it. He don't like killing. After it was done, he pulled her up by the house and salvaged what he could of the meat. Now let's talk about me," he said with a smile. "Sometimes I like to, sometimes I don't. Son, I'm old. The best I can recall, this is my twenty-third summer. I grew up with Mr. Pete. I don't hear like I used to Son. My eyes aren't as good as they used to be. I have outlived every old dog in the county." He laughed. "You see I don't get around like I used to. One of these days I'll hardly be able to walk at all. I already lost my teeth, but I can still smell good enough. No self respecting farm dog wants to get to where he can't do anything for himself. If I ever get that way it would sure be kind of Mr. Bill to let me die. I hope that young pup learns well enough so I can go knowing that the farm is still in good paws."

Clutch asked, "Will Mr. Bill eat you?"

Drowser howled with laughter. "No Son. Anyone trying to eat this old dog will lose their teeth trying. I won't even make good jerky. The Dobsins have a special place on this farm to bury their faithful loved ones. You know that old apple tree in the meadow that I go to often? They'll put me in the ground there beside my mate. If I know our humans like I think I do, they'll all get wet eyed and spend the next two weeks talking about the good times. Tell me Son, what could be better than that?" Drowser turned his head to the sky again.

Out of curiosity Clutch asked, "What are you watching up there?"

Drowser answered with a smile, "All of it Son. I've been looking up there for twenty-three years."

"But why?" inquired Clutch.

Drowser replied, "Two reasons. The first is that it's pretty. The other is because it's there and I can see it. I don't know what's behind it, but I've come to figure just that it's there and I can see it. If I ever get to where my eyes don't work, I can still see it with my mind." Before Clutch could ask another question Drowser barked, "Run along Son. Go get some sleep."

As Clutch was leaving he affectionately rubbed against the old dog. He then returned to the others.

Brenda and Pete were down to one last name and number on their list.

"Let's see," said Brenda, "out of nineteen calls we have fourteen relatives who will definitely be here."

Pete said "One left on the list."

"Aunt Clara," they both answered together.

As Brenda reached for the phone it rang.

"Hello. Is this Brenda Kingman?"

Brenda replied, "Yes. How may I help you?"

"Brenda, this is Crystal from Jersey. Do you remember me?"

She responded, "Yes. What can I do for you?"

Crystal asked, "Remember our little contest with the kittens?"

Brenda said, "Yes. Are they gonna be in the calendar?"

"Absolutely," replied Crystal. "We posted the pictures that we accumulated on our website. The contest ended at midnight on Friday. We have a problem though. It seems that Clutch and Calli are tied for first place. How are we going to decide this? My husband proposes putting the kittens together in the same picture and splitting the prize between you and Pete. I wanted to call you and ask if that would be all right. We've never had this happen before."

Brenda laughed heartily. "It's certainly fine by me. Pete's right here. Should I ask him or do you want to?"

Crystal answered, "Since he's right there go ahead and ask him."

Brenda told Pete what was happening. He laughed and gave his okay.

"Honey, you might as well give her the rest of the story," Pete told Brenda.

Brenda responded, "It's fine by him, but there's something you should know. Pete and I are getting married."

Crystal exclaimed, "Well now, perhaps a little help with a check will give you a great start. There's a little more. We'd like to make arrangements to hand deliver the check. If it's all right, maybe we could take a few more pictures."

Brenda replied, "I don't know when Pete and I can get back through to New Jersey."

Crystal said, "We're gonna be coming through Indianapolis on the way to Chicago for a cat show. The show doesn't start until the fifteenth. We like to take about two days to set up, and we have an appointment in Indianapolis on the ninth with one of our suppliers. Will you and Pete be available on that weekend?"

Brenda relayed all of this to Pete and they both roared with laughter.

Brenda casually replied to Crystal, "Oh, we'll be in that weekend, but we have plans for Saturday the tenth. Our plans, however, definitely leave room for guests. Join us."

Crystal inquired, "Is it a party? I love parties."

Brenda sounded amused. "Yes."

Crystal continued, "What's the occasion? Tell us when and where to show up and we'll be there."

Brenda smiled, "It's a lot of things all rolled up into one. It's taking place at Wendover Trucking."

Crystal blurted, "Delightful! I love attending tax write-offs...I mean parties. What's going on?"

Brenda carefully replied, "Oh, nothing much. At 11 o'clock there will be a safety meeting. There will be some games and a retirement party for Dad, and our wedding."

Crystal was startled. "What did you say?"

Brenda quipped, "Oops. I forgot about the BBQ."

Crystal said, "Whoa Girl. Back up a bit. This party is actually for your wedding? You're inviting us to your wedding at the terminal?"

Brenda didn't hesitate. "Absolutely. Clutch and Calli will be part of the wedding."

Crystal, for the first time in her life, was speechless. Finally she said, "I'm not even going to ask Edwin. We'll be there. How about free pictures for the wedding as our contribution?"

Brenda conferred with Pete and they both agreed that it would be wonderful.

Crystal added, "I'll tell my husband to pack all of his gear. He's quite the photographer you know."

Brenda replied, "That would be great Crystal. Thank you very much."

She answered, "I can't wait to tell Edwin. Who knows, maybe we'll do a second calendar with just them. We'll see you two at the wedding, er, BBQ. Bye now."

As Brenda was about to dial her Aunt Clara for a second time,

Pete refilled their coffee cups. "The bottom of the pot," he laughed. "I think we need this."

Brenda dialed her Great Aunt's phone number. "Aunt Clara, this is Brenda Kingman. How are you today?"

Aunt Clara answered, "I'm fine Dear. I'm so happy to hear from you so soon. Are you all right? How is your father?"

Brenda replied, "Dad's fine. I just wanted to thank you for such a lovely visit."

Aunt Clara responded, "You are most certainly welcome. I love surprises, especially good ones. How is that handsome young man you brought along? If you ask me Dear, you better sink your hooks into him quick. Don't let him get away."

Brenda said, "Aunt Clara, Pete's right here. Would you like to talk to him?"

Aunt Clara replied, "I'd be delighted. Maybe I'll give him another dose. Go ahead and put him on."

Brenda handed the phone to Pete.

"Hello Mrs. Snyder," Pete said.

She replied, "Dear, please call me Aunt Clara."

He said, "Okay, Aunt Clara. It seems to me that I made a promise to you. Brenda and I have decided to drink from that cup. We want you and your family there when we do. Do you and your husband have plans for the tenth?"

Aunt Clara asked, "Dear, what are you getting at? I'm not entirely sure we're on the same page."

Pete replied, "Aunt Clara, Brenda and I are getting married in Indianapolis on the tenth. If at all possible, we would be honored if your family would be there. If you come a few days early, maybe

Uncle Wes could go fishing with me in the ponds, if you don't have other plans that is. Brenda is staying at my farm. Perhaps we should have a chaperone."

Through her tears, Aunt Clara quickly accepted.

Pete said, "I'll hand the phone back over to Brenda. She can fill you in. Just let us know when to expect you. We'll have everything set up."

Brenda talked briefly with her aunt, about forty-five minutes, and then they said their fifteen-minute goodbyes.

Calli was enjoying herself, strolling around the farm, telling everyone that would listen how proud she was of herself for catching three mice in her first night.

On her way out to the pasture to tell Boots and the diary girls of her accomplishments she heard a strange voice say, "Well, if it's not the patchwork mouse killer. HA!HA!HA!"

Calli was startled. "Who are you? Who said that?" she demanded as se sniffed the air. All she could smell was the barn scrapings.

"Let me guess," continued the strange voice. "Your very first night and you killed three mice. Big deal."

Calli looked around and could see no one. She hissed, "That's right! I killed three mice in my first night." Calli sat down with her chest puffed out. "If you're not careful, I might just dig into you."

The cruel voice growled with laughter. "So you think, Little Girl."

At first Calli could not see who was talking to her. Then she saw a large animal, larger than her, coming from the cement blocks that encased the manure pile.

Its long sleek body was standing up to make sure they were alone. "You silly Lap Kitty! Let me tell you about accomplishments. Why in the last year alone I've helped myself to lots and lots of eggs—too many to count. Why bother? I take what I want. I've killed at least ten chickens just because I wanted to. I love the taste of fresh chicken."

Calli growled, "What kind of animal are you? You look like a mouse, a big one."

Again the animal laughed harshly. "HA!HA!HA! You don't even know a rat when you see one Missy? You think you have teeth? Look at these!" He bared his sharp fangs that smelled strangely of death. "Let me finish telling you of my accomplishments. In the last year alone I've killed nine kittens and puppies, all of which get blamed on stray tomcats. There's even rumor going around that it's the oversized, not so Great Tom Cat of the Woods. You know Furball, that nutcase of a farmer just got done harvesting wheat. I was just thinking how good fresh wheat tastes." The rat circled Calli with an evil grin. "You know what would make that wheat taste even better?"

Calli was starting to feel afraid.

"Kitten blood in my mouth. That would really enhance the flavor of the grain. Wouldn't that be a big blow to Miss Tabby, losing her star pupil? What a tasty thought."

Calli growled again. "I'll bite you!"

The rat laughed menacingly. "Girly, I'm going to enjoy killing you. I've been doing this for three years. Nobody even knows I'm here! All they smell is manure! One from our family has been in this very place for more than twelve years. It was my own grandfather that killed the old furbag Sally's kittens. Got all but one of them. He'd have gotten the last one too, but she came back too soon dragging that bobcat kitten she stole. You think it's an accomplishment that you killed three mice in one night? He killed five kittens in one hour, while they were still sucking milk. Just imagine how poor Miss Tabby and that freak tomcat kitten will feel seeing your destroyed body lying here. Well, enough talk Bone Bag."

As the rat lunged at Calli, Clutch jumped from out of nowhere and landed on top of his body, sinking his claws into the rat's body and his teeth into the back of his neck. The rat tried to throw Clutch off and escape but could not. The more he struggled, the deeper Clutch's fangs sank into his neck.

Calli screamed in distress.

All over the farm animals came running to the rescue. Even the Great Tom Cat of the Woods himself came running from the woods.

Miss Tabby arrived first. The rat's body was still twitching with death.

As the other animals arrived they started cheering for Clutch, for no kitten had ever before killed a rat on the farm.

The loud noises of the animals attracted the attention of Bill Dobsin. He came to see what the commotion was. He let out a whoop of delight and ran inside to brag to his wife. "Mae! You'll never guess what I just saw!" He told her of what Clutch had done. "I bet that darned thing weighs three pounds!"

Aunt Mae smiled. "Maybe that's what's been stealing our eggs and killing our chickens! Pete will sure be glad to hear this!"

The roar of applause continued for quite a while.

Clutch still held on.

Tabby said encouragingly, "You did well Son. We are all very proud of you."

Clutch did not seem to hear her. Silence fell over the group of animals, but Clutch still held onto the rat. Even when the Great Tom Cat called his name three times it was as if no one spoke at all.

Again Calli was fearful, but this time for Clutch. She cautiously walked beside him and placed her paw on his shoulder. "It's all right Clutch. He's dead. Everything is fine now."

Clutch slowly came back to reality and released the rat's limp body. "He was going to kill Calli. He said he killed nine puppies and kittens. He bragged about killing ten chickens and stealing eggs. He was going to kill Calli!"

The Great Tom Cat spoke, "Son, you did very well. You put an end to many tragedies. You have solved many of the problems and heartbreaks this farm has seen. You did what no kitten has done. No tomcat could ever be more proud of their son than I am of you."

All of the animals cheered loudly again. As they celebrated Clutch silently slipped away.

A little while later Calli found Clutch sitting beside the pond where he had washed the redness off of his face. Calli rubbed her head against his shoulder, purring loudly. "I thought your Pete was my biggest hero. You saved my life."

Clutch sighed. "I don't know what happened to me back there, Calli. One minute I heard him saying all of those awful things, then all I remember is you telling me it was over."

Calli gently replied, "You did a very wonderful thing, Clutch. It is the most wonderful thing any kitten has ever done here. You saved my life."

Clutch exclaimed, "I couldn't let him hurt you! I wouldn't!"

Calli started licking the corner of his mouth.

Clutch meowed, "The red stuff? Did I miss some?"

Calli giggled, "No. I just wanted to give you a thank you kiss."

Clutch was embarrassed, but kissed her back.

"Come on Hero. Let's go back to the others. By the way Clutch, I overheard Mae Dobsin on the phone. I gotta tell you, she's real proud of you. I don't know who she was talking to, but she said she's taking all of the leftovers out and giving them to the cats."

Clutch spat. "Maybe some food will help get that nasty taste out of my mouth."

Calli challenged, "Come on Hero! I'll race you."

As Clutch and Calli rounded the corner by the back porch Mrs. Dobsin had a big pot she was banging on.

She hollered, "Come and get it!" Then she saw Clutch. She bent down to scratch his ears and shoulders, then reached into the pot and pulled out a big chunk of beef fat. She smiled. "This is for you!" She dumped the rest of the contents for all of the animals.

Drowser barked, "Lord, I haven't seen a feast like this in a long while!"

Every day Pete and Brenda spent as much time as they could with their kittens as they prepared for the upcoming wedding.

Although Clutch was such a celebrity on the farm, he would sneak away for some time alone whenever he could. No one would question where he went or follow him. He always went to the same place on the backside of the pond.

One night, as the last rays of the setting sun darkened into night, Clutch was looking up at the stars when a familiar voice behind him said, "They're really quite pretty, aren't they Son?"

It was the Great Tom Cat himself.

Clutch answered, "Yes Sir. They are quite beautiful."

The larger cat asked, "Being a hero doesn't set very well with you, does it Clutch?"

Clutch hung his head. "I don't know how I feel Sir."

The Great Tom Cat sat beside him. "As you already know Clutch, I am your father. I must say your spots are coming in very nicely."

Clutch smiled, "Thank you Sir."

"Clutch," he started, "what is it like to travel in a truck?"

Clutch replied, "It's wonderful. My Pete-human shows me so

many new things. He showed me this big pond that he says has no fish in it and another place where, as far as you can see, it's one giant litter box. I get to taste different things. I even make sure his coffee and chili are good. We get to taste all kinds of different meats like crab, shrimp, and something called swordfish." Clutch paused. "I guess things have changed now. Everyone will expect me to be the hero. I never killed anything before."

The Great Tom Cat took his massive paw and rubbed the fur on Clutch's head.

Clutch mewed, "And I guess everyone will expect me to stay here now."

The older tomcat asked, "Why? Why should you? Do you want to stay here? Do you understand that your two humans, Pete and Brenda, after they are bonded and leave out together, will expect you to go along? You belong with them, you and Calli both."

"I know," Clutch said, "but the others will still expect me to stay."

The Great Tom Cat looked down at his son with that ever-present smile. "Son, my birth mother gave birth to me right there in the Dobsin kitchen. Mother Sally gave me her milk and weaned me. Brother Drowser taught me everything he could think of to be a part of this farm. Your Peter carried me around, played with me like I was his pet. Miss Mae even swatted me with her broom for chasing the chickens, and Mr. Bill thinks nothing of it when I take a little milk from the pan. I live in the woods, but this farm is still a part of my home. Just this past spring a pretty female bobcat wanted me to leave this place and go deep into the woods where there are plenty of rabbits and mice. I told her no. This is where I choose to be. No matter how often you may go away with your Pete-human, you and he will always come back. This is your home and his. We are all Dobsins. This is the Dobsin farm. We are not just animals here. If your heart tells you to go, you should go. If your heart tells you to stay, you should stay. You are my son. You must never settle for anything less than what is in your heart."

Clutch purred, "Calli and I belong with Pete and Brenda."

The Great Tom Cat gently said, "Then go where you belong. When you come back, tell us what you have seen out there. We will all sit quietly and listen anxiously. You are a trucking cat. Don't ever forget that."

"Father, Mr. Pete and Miss Brenda want Calli and me to be part of their wedding."

"Do you want to?" asked the Great Tom Cat.

Clutch purred, "Yes. Calli and I both want to."

The Great Tom Cat laughed. "Then do it. You can tell us all about it."

Clutch smiled at his father and said with pride, "We will."

The Great Tom Cat grinned. "Who knows, Son. Maybe one of these days you and I will go to the woods together to hunt. I don't know about you, but I'm going back by the house. Mrs. Dobsin just poured another pot of food, including a big chunk of roast beef."

Clutch smiled at the Great Tom Cat. "I'm up for that challenge."

The Great Tom Cat laughed, "Rabbit is good, but this is easier to catch."

* * *

That evening, after everyone had gorged themselves again on Miss Mae's generosity, the animals were all together begging of Clutch, "Tell us again how you killed that rat!"

Calli sat beside Clutch openly admiring him.

Clutch looked at everyone for a long while before he answered. "It's not really all that good of a feeling. I did nothing special. Calli was in trouble. She needed help. I did nothing more than what any of you would have done. I came to the aid of someone I care about. We're a family here. We protect each other because we love each other.

The animals went silent.

The Great Tom Cat spoke next. "And that, Clutch, is who and what we are, a community, a family. Do you know what I would like to hear about, Clutch? Please tell us about the big pond with no fish."

Clutch replied, "My Pete-human calls it the 'Great Salt Lake.' If you sit on top of the big hill and look at it from a distance you can see where it starts and ends. People that live there drive their cars like a nest of stirred up hornets. When they crash into each other they blame the other person for not watching. The roads look like a big nest of ants going in every which direction but don't seem to be going anywhere." He continued on for a few more moments and then went silent. After a while, while everyone was talking among themselves, Clutch and Calli got up to leave.

One of Della's puppies, Spike, barked, "Hey! Kwutch, where are ya' goin'?"

This time Calli answered. "Spike, Clutch and I need to go home."

Sassy, one of Clutch's sisters, blurted out, "This is home!"

Calli replied, "It's part of our home, but we also belong with Pete and Brenda. The farm is a big place. And do you really think humans can plan something as important as a wedding without us to supervise?"

Clutch smiled. "Yup. Everything is getting back to normal."

Tabby was about to call out a warning but the Great Tom Cat turned and simply licked her ear. She gave a worried look to the Great Tom Cat, but he sat there and smiled.

Tabby's tensions eased and she rolled over onto her back to bat at his chin with her paws.

After Clutch and Calli blended into the darkness Della suggested that she take two of her cadets and follow them to make sure they arrived safely.

Drowser barked, "Stand down, Girl. They'll be fine."

* * *

Pete and Brenda were sitting on the porch swing together when Clutch and Calli leapt onto the porch.

Pete looked down at the kittens and said, "Well Dear, we can't very well say, 'Look what the cat dragged in.' now can we?"

Brenda laughed. "Come here you two."

In a single jump the kittens were on their laps.

After giving their humans hugs they curled up on their laps just purring away.

Brenda squeezed Pete's hand. "The family's all together."

The following morning, after helping with the milking, the four adults sat down for breakfast.

Pete had a busy day lined up.

"Let's see," said Brenda. "Today is Friday. Eight days to go."

Pete smiled. "An eternity if you ask me."

Brenda added, "Pete, Aunt Mae and I are going to be busy this afternoon. If you need me though, I can change plans."

Pete insisted, "Nah, you two girls go have fun. I need to go to the bank, and then I need to go to Lafayette for a few hours. Are we still having a party out here Sunday afternoon? Like a reunion?"

Brenda answered, "Well, we agreed on it, but it's not set in stone." She looked concerned.

"I still want to. I haven't changed my mind. I just figured that since I'm going to Lafayette anyway I can pick up a lot of stuff now and save a trip later," said Pete.

Brenda agreed. "I'm sorry Dear. I'm just a little jittery. Oops! I forgot something. We've agreed to house as many relatives as we can at the house. We've gotta get the house cleaned."

Aunt Mae cut in. "I've got that covered Kids. There's a half dozen ladies at the church wanting to snoop into your house anyway. A couple of phone calls and I'll have a cleaning crew together. Of course, Brenda, get yourself prepared to be bombarded with questions."

Brenda smiled. "Pete, while you're in town will you please pick me up some mint tea bags? I think I'm going to need them."

Pete said, "I've got you covered, at least on the tea bags."

"Honey, I promised to take Grandpa in to town today. He won't tell me what for though. He just said he had an appointment with his attorney."

Pete replied, "Okay. Tell your grandpa I said hi and I'm sorry I didn't get in to see him."

Brenda added, "Oh, I forgot something else. He said he wants to know when you two are going fishing. He says he's got the taste of fresh trout in his mouth."

Pete responded, "Tell him I'll call him and we'll go fishing together in a couple of days."

"I'm going to get all of the cat toys out of the truck so we can sort through them."

Brenda agreed. "We can probably use some of that stuff for the wedding."

Pete smiled and nodded. "Just what I was thinking."

Brenda's cell phone rang. It was Aunt Clara.

"Hi Brenda. This is Aunt Clara. Did I call at a bad time?"

"No," said Brenda. "How are you doing?"

"I'm fine Dear. Your Uncle Wes and I are coming out about a week early. I haven't spoken to my brother-in-law since, well, let's just say it's been a long time. Could you be a dear and set up a motel room for us? It's been such a long time, and I don't remember the name of the place."

Brenda answered, "Hold on a minute Aunt Clara. Let me speak with Pete real quick."

Brenda explained the situation to Pete and he said, "Tell them to come out to the house. Remind Uncle Wes to bring his rods."

Brenda told her aunt and gave her directions to Pete's house. She then asked, "When will you be in the area?"

Her aunt replied, "We'll be there tomorrow evening. It's been a long time since we've visited that beautiful chapel, only last time it wasn't so pleasant. And I want to spend some time with your grandpa. I promised him I'd stay in touch, but it was just too hard to make the call."

Brenda's eyes were filling up with tears. "I understand Aunt Clara."

Aunt Clara insisted, "Well Dear, I'm sure you have more important things to do than talk to an old crow. I'll see you soon. Bye."

Brenda wiped her eyes.

Pete kissed her and retreated out the door.

Aunt Mae asked Brenda, "Shall I make a dress for Calli?"

Brenda smiled. "No thank you. If you would like to, come over and look at the stuff for the cats from California and New Jersey. I'm going to pick out something from that for them to wear for the wedding."

Aunt Mae laughed. "It sounds like fun. I've never picked out clothing for a cat before."

* * *

Pete set up the litter pan in the pantry and, after bringing in four large bags of cat supplies, laid Clutch's blanket on a worn chest in his bedroom. He took a long look at the kittens, especially Clutch. He said to himself, "He's getting more and more spots every day. I don't have to wonder who his daddy is." He said to the kittens, "I hate to tell you this, but you two are getting your shots at the same time. The vet is coming out on Monday to bring supplies." Pete thought about taking the kittens with him in to town but decided against it. "Okay you two, you've got guard duty. I'll take care of you when I get home." He hopped into his pickup and headed in to town.

First Pete went to the bank to deposit his settlement check from Wendover and the check he received from the sale of his calves. After numerous congratulations and pats on the back for his upcoming marriage, he was more than glad to be back in his pickup and on his way to Lafayette, Indiana.

When all of his business was finally done, he was glad to be back home again with the kittens.

Brenda said, "Pete, I talked to Vonell and there are thirty-four who accommodations will be made for. You said we'll open up rooms in the house and you and I will be getting a room at a hotel Saturday. How many rooms in the house will be available?"

Pete thought for a moment. "We have three rooms available before Saturday, including the sewing room. Saturday night my room will be empty."

Brenda responded, "The master bedroom won't be used Saturday. We'll be at the hotel."

"Nah," said Pete with a grin. "Let's keep that one open."

Brenda smiled. "You're a beast!" Brenda continued, "Aunt Mae has offered three more rooms to be available. Grandpa has even offered three rooms to be opened up for the Kingman family. He says he won't have it any other way. He said that he has been silent for too many years. Pete, he even wants Mom and Dad to stay there. To quote his words he said, 'It's time for two tomcats to get together without shedding fur.'"

Pete replied, "I don't want to be that much a burden to your grandfather. It's a very generous offer but…"

Brenda interrupted, "Burden? Pete, I've never seen him this excited about anything! Part of the business we did today was hiring a cleaning service to clean the house from attic to basement. Pete, he even bought a new gas range. It has six burners and two ovens."

Pete's eyes widened. "Make sure to tell him we'll reimburse him for all the expenses, even the oven."

Brenda shot back, "I don't think so. He said if you show up with a checkbook, or even pull your wallet out, he's gonna tan your hide like he did last time. By the way, what did he do that for?"

Pete's ears turned red. "He saw me kiss you while we were stacking hay. He told me he wouldn't tell your daddy. He figured he'd tanned me enough for the both of them."

Brenda asked, "Did he?"

Pete smiled, "I think he got me enough for every member of the Kingman family and then some."

They both laughed.

Brenda went on, "He asked if Aunt Clara and Uncle Wes were coming. When I told him yes his reply was, 'the sister of a Kingman wife is a Kingman.' He was very insistent. It would really hurt his pride if it was any other way."

Pete nodded in understanding. "Hey Brenda, do you think your grandfather would tan my hide if he saw me kiss you before the wedding?"

Brenda smiled dangerously. "Well let's see, he might, but I promise you that if you don't risk it I will."

Pete leaned in and kissed her lightly.

Brenda changed the subject. "Okay, now back to what we need to take care of. The hotel is reserving the entire blue wing at the company price so long as everyone is checked in by 5 o'clock on Friday or calls ahead. Anyone that does not call or check in by 5 o'clock pays full price with no guarantee of an available room."

Pete smiled. "Good thing it's not a race week!"

They both laughed.

Pete asked, "Brenda, why don't we invite your grandfather over for dinner. We can both pick him up. He'll have to bring his fishing pole though. As a matter of fact, we'll catch dinner."

Brenda smiled, "I know that will work. He's been wanting to have a little chat with you privately. He says he knows you have the right stuff but wants to make sure you wear it."

Pete teased, "Do you think he wants me to learn about the birds and the bees?"

Brenda laughed, "Probably. Drink your coffee. It's getting cold."

Pete added, "By the way, I'm having 150 pounds of ice delivered for Sunday. They're just gonna bring out a freezer full and put it out in the tool shed."

Brenda replied, "I forgot about ice. You think of everything don't you?"

Pete continued, "Since neither of us drink alcohol, I ordered ten cases of each sparkling white grape, sparkling cherry, and sparkling cranberry—something for everyone, plus a pickup full of sodas, fresh brewed iced tea, and Aunt Mae's thirty-cup coffee urn."

Brenda shook her head, "You really do think of everything. Where are we spending our wedding night?"

Pete answered, "I don't want to decide that by myself. What would you like to do?"

Brenda replied, "I know of a place not far from here that would be a great little hide-away. No one would think of it. I seem to remember helping a certain young man build a small cabin in a pretty thick patch of woods before basic training. He said something like, 'A grown man should live under his own roof.'"

Pete responded, "That cabin is still available. I think all it will need is a good cleaning. I'll look into it tomorrow morning after milking."

Brenda grinned, "It will be perfect."

"On to the other stuff. Tomorrow afternoon at 5 o'clock LeyAnn and Millie are coming out with their dresses. Aunt Mae is doing touch-ups on something else we're getting together."

Pete said, "I'm going to the attic tomorrow to see what I can find in the boxes, maybe restore some old memories."

Brenda nodded her head. "Aunt Mae even talked about making a dress for Calli."

Pete smiled, "Why not? She is a girl. Let the whole bridal party hang together."

Brenda said, "Rob wants to see you at about 6 o'clock tomorrow evening in his office."

Pete whistled, "Six o'clock this Saturday? Maybe I better put off going to the attic. If you don't mind I'll just take Clutch with me tomorrow to Indy and have a little guy time."

Brenda replied, "I think that's a wonderful idea."

The following morning, after milking and breakfast, Uncle Bill volunteered to go with Pete. They'd work together to clean that cabin.

Aunt Mae chipped in, "Like men know anything about cleaning."

Uncle Bill smiled and shrugged his shoulders. "If you remember correctly, I do it everyday out in the barn. Hey Pete, mind if I ride along with you in to the city today? Brenda's Aunt Clara called and said it would be late when they get in. She said they had a slight change of plans. She said she called Tom, Sr. He wants them to stay over there. We'll meet up with them in church tomorrow. Let's get goin' Son. We'll probably need to put a little grease on that old well pump while we're there. There's no telling how much work we're gonna have up there."

They headed up to the cabin.

When Pete opened the door a flood of memories came rushing at him all at once, along with two raccoons. The two men walked in looking around.

Bill said, "Well now, there's not a whole lot needin' done after all, Son."

Pete looked around. "Are you sure this is my place?"

"Yeah," replied Uncle Bill. "I came over a couple of days ago. I thought you might like to have a hide-away. The table came out of the old butcher house. I made sure it was scrubbed first. I got the two chairs out of there too. I don't know if you're old enough to remember that bed or not. I've been storing it in the smokehouse for a long while."

Pete was astonished at the brass single bed.

"The mattress and box spring are new. I replaced the chimney pipe. I went to clean the woodstove, but those two raccoons didn't seem interested in leaving."

Pete gave his uncle a hug and then the two men sat down.

Bill continued, "Son, I don't know what to do anymore. Your dad already had a talk with you about the birds and the bees. Here you are, all grown up, fixin' to start a family of your own." The aging man wiped his face with a flannel shirtsleeve. "I don't know what kind of gift to get you for your wedding. I don't know what you need, but I do know you. Your Aunt Mae and I signed papers. When it's time for us to go and be with your parents, everything is yours. The papers were done in a way that you won't even have to pay inheritance tax. There's more than enough life insurance to cover any debts we might have at that time. All this land has belonged to the Dobsin family for over 120 years. The only line we put on the property between your daddy and me was on paper. Pete and I were brothers right up until his last breath. You've always been like a son to me. When our little county chapel was built, a Dobsin put the first stone block in place. I hope one day it can be said that nobody owned this land but a Dobsin. Son, what I'm trying to get at is that

I love you and I couldn't be more proud of you if you were my son. You've had eyes for that girl since you were eight. Mae and I are so happy for you." Getting up and wiping his eyes he finished, "Let's grease that pump before we forget."

Before Uncle Bill could make his way to the door, Pete hugged him again.

* * *

On their way into Indianapolis, Pete teased his uncle, "I thought you hated Indy."

His uncle shrugged his shoulders and said, "I do. I just wanted to spend the day with you."

Pete replied, "I'm mighty glad to have you with me. As a matter of fact, let's go to the men's store at the mall. Your suit coat is startin' to look a little shiny with age. Let's see what we can do about that."

Uncle Bill scratched his chin. "I wouldn't say it's all that old. It's only been twenty years. It's just now gettin' broke in. Don't tell me leisure suits are out of style."

Both men laughed.

Uncle Bill asked, "Is Mae in on this?"

"No," answered Pete. "I do know that Brenda and the girls are taking her into Lafayette to get her a new dress though."

Bill asked, "How are we going to keep you two apart before the wedding? The groom's not supposed to see the dress before the wedding."

Pete replied, "I think Brenda's already got that figured out, Uncle

Bill. On Friday, when the girls get together again, Millie Wendover is gonna take the dress back to the office and Rob is gonna take my tux. He'll pick it up Thursday. The women's restroom in the new trailer shed is gonna be marked 'Out of Service.' The women will change in there. The men will dress in the trailer shed office. While Jimmy is getting everyone's attention Rose will see that all the special guests are seated. While Jimmy is leading everyone in a word of prayer Millie and LeyAnn will take their places, as will Broadus and Rob. When Jim finishes his prayer and calls for the band to play, they'll launch immediately into the 'Wedding March.' Brenda and I will head down the side together with Calli and Clutch. Brenda's wedding band will be attached by a clip to a bow tie on Clutch's collar. Calli will carry my ring secured with a ribbon on her hat."

Bill declared, "You're really keeping this hush-hush, aren't you Son? Ain't it kind of hard to keep secrets at a trucking company?"

Pete laughed. "Vonell made it very clear to everyone in the office that if anybody tells anyone about the secret they'll answer to her."

"From what I understand," said Uncle Bill, "I don't think our new service bull would want to lock horns with her."

Pete added, "Rob did tell two other people outside of the office. It wouldn't be right not to tell the head mechanic what his new trailer shop was being used for. His wife is the tow truck operator. They promised not to tell anyone, but they wouldn't anyway."

Uncle Bill just shook his head.

"It sounds like it's well planned out. Who would believe it was put together in less than two weeks? Are Tommy and Phyllis still in Hawaii?"

"Yup," answered Pete. "They'll get back into Indy on

Wednesday, a few days before the wedding. Brenda has already taken Phyllis's dress to the cleaners. As soon as Tom and Phyllis get in they're going straight to Tom, Sr.'s house."

"If Phyllis's dress needs to be altered at all," Uncle Bill cut in, "There'll be enough lady beavers to rebuild her a new one in a day."

As they were pulling into the mall parking lot Pete said, "You know, I just thought of something Mom told me before I shipped out to basic. Since she never had a daughter her wedding dress was to go to Brenda. She said she left that to Aunt Mae, though."

Bill gave his nephew an astonished look. "I'm not saying nothin' other than 'something old, something new, something borrowed, and…'"

"Something blue," the two men said together smiling.

* * *

By 4 o'clock the two men were returning to the pickup with Bill Dobsin carrying two suits.

As the men climbed into the vehicle, Uncle Bill held up his catch and said, "Don't tell the cows about this. They might want me to wear it in the milk barn." He looked at his watch and said, "Son, I think we missed lunch. Why don't we stop on our way and grab a bite. I'll buy. I'm in the mood for chilidogs. Mae would skin me alive if she found out I was eating them."

The men proceeded to wolf down some chilidogs and fries, washing them down with a couple bottles of cola each.

"Now don't tell your aunt about this."

Pete promised to keep their secret.

At 5:45 they pulled into the parking lot of Wendover Trucking and walked into the drivers' lounge.

Pete looked in his pigeon box and saw a piece of paper. The note read, "Come on back to the conference room. The doors are unlocked." Pete opened the door and walked through with Uncle Bill behind him. He knocked on the door of the conference room and heard, 'Come in.'

When Pete opened the door he saw about twenty men standing there, all of whom he recognized. They were all retired drivers who had driven with his father.

Rob looked at Bill with a smile and said, "Thank you for keeping him delayed for us. It wouldn't be right for the guest of honor to be the first to arrive to his own party."

Over the next couple of hours, all of the other men told their stories and memories of driving with Pete, Sr., then they shared a picture with Pete as a piece of memorabilia of his father.

At 7 o'clock the phone rang.

Rob answered it then excused himself from the party. When he returned twenty minutes later, there were three men with him carrying boxes that contained chilidogs, french fries, pizzas, cherry pie, and apple pie. Everyone was quite contented.

Pete would not hide his emotions from these men, for they all knew him far too well. He turned to Uncle Bill and asked, "How did you know about this?"

Rob answered for him. "Your uncle called me Wednesday morning. This was all his idea. He said he wanted to set it up at his house, but he couldn't do it without you finding out about it. I'll tell you what. Your uncle is a true Dobsin. He is one stubborn fellow.

He said it was his party and wouldn't let me pay a penny toward it. All I had to do was call up your dad's friends."

One of the men pulled a bottle out of his pocket. Every man took a taste as a tribute to Pete's mother and father. It was not soda pop.

Pete wiped the tears from his face realizing these men were not his dad's friends they were his family. They all had the same last name—Wendover Trucking.

Pete announced that at his wedding these men and their wives would all be seated to the front, as Pete's uncles, the brothers of his father.

As the community bottle was passed around the second and final time Pete simply wiped the tears from his face and proclaimed, "No man could have a better group of uncles than this."

Most of the men wiped the tears from their own faces.

The party was over by 9 o'clock and everyone went home.

Wednesday at 10 o'clock Pete and Brenda stood hand in hand as her parents' plane taxied into the terminal.

As Tom and Phyllis stepped off the plane they embraced Pete and Brenda. Phyllis and Brenda immediately started crying.

Tom wiped his own eyes and said to a flight attendant, "You better get maintenance up here with lots of buckets. These two are fixin' to have a flood." Tom looked at his daughter and asked, "Okay, since everyone is making these arrangements, what are we doing next and were are we doing it?"

Brenda replied, "Gramps insists that you and Mom stay there until the wedding."

Tom gave his daughter a surprised look. "Dad wants us to stay with him? He didn't fall and butt his head on something did he?"

Brenda gave her father a sharp look but said nothing.

Phyllis gave her husband's hand a squeeze.

Tom smiled, "It will be good to see Dad again. We might even have something to talk about. I know Dad hates company." Tom was even more surprised to learn that his father had opened his home for relatives to stay.

Pete and Tom took the front seats of Pete's '65 T-Bird so that

Brenda and her mother could converse over the most recent events. Tom leaned over and whispered to Pete, "Do you, by chance, have a weed whacker?"

Pete answered, "I sure do. Why?"

Tom responded, "Phyllis bought Brenda an authentic grass skirt."

When his wife overheard his comments he covered his steps by adding, "Uh, I might need it to do some trim work around my house."

Everyone laughed.

As they pulled into the Kingman's Farm driveway Tom tensed up and said, "I haven't been back here since Mom... Let's just say it's been a while. Pete, if things don't go well, I mean, if I need a little break, mind if I try a little fishing?"

Pete smiled, "I keep all the fishing gear on the back porch. Everything you could want or need is there except for live bait. You'll have to find that on your own."

Tom said, "Well, don't be surprised if I camp out by the pond."

That evening Aunt Clara cooked up a feast at the Kingman home. Everyone, Kingman or Dobsin, was expected to be there. Tom and his father had not spoken much, other than to say they were glad to see each other.

After dinner Tom, Jr. excused himself and stepped out onto the back porch to reminisce.

About fifteen minutes later, his father emerged from the kitchen and asked, "Tommy, can you give me a hand down at the smokehouse? Pete's throwing a shin-dig at his place Sunday afternoon and I told him he could use some of my wash tubs to chill drinks in."

Tom did not verbally answer his father but nodded his head and followed him.

They flipped on the light switch as they entered the small smokehouse. As Tom, Sr. closed the door behind him he said, "Son, I just wanted a chance to talk to you alone for a few minutes. I haven't been the best dad to you. I know I said a lot of things I didn't mean and a lot of mean things. But it's what I didn't say that hurts the most. What I wanted to say, I was too stubborn to."

Tom Kingman, Jr. said nothing but continued to listen to his father.

"What I'm trying to tell you, Son, is how much I love you and how proud I am of you. When your Momma died, I realized just how much I wish there was a magic pill that would take all these years of hurt away."

Tom embraced his father in a hug for a long moment. When he finally pulled away he said, "That's the magic pill that takes hurt away. I just wish we had something to wash them down with."

Tom, Jr. was totally astonished when the aged man opened the refrigerator door, produced two bottles of amber colored liquid, and handed one to his son.

"Momma wouldn't let me keep it in the house."

As the two men enjoyed each other's company Tom, Jr. said, "You know Pop, Pete's got that pond with trout over there. Why don't we slip over there and catch some trout for breakfast?"

The old man smiled and tapped his glass container with a withered fingertip. "Let's see if I can find a couple more of these to take with us."

Phyllis could only smile when she saw her husband and his father walking back towards the house with their arms over each other's shoulders. After all, what more needed to be said?

* * *

The following morning Pete emerged from the milk house with the intent of calling the Kingman house to invite his future father-in-law, his father, and Uncle Wes over to his place to catch trout. As he stepped onto his aunt and uncle's back porch he noticed the two men fishing in his trout pond. He said to himself, "Why don't I invite Uncle Wes to go fishing for bass? I'm sure he would love to come along." He didn't want to go near the two men at the trout pond.

By 8 o'clock all five men were standing around an open fire roasting their fish. They talked about whatever came to mind. Pete opened a cooler and produced several cans of ice-cold soda. The men, engaged in deep conversation, occasionally looked over their shoulders to make sure the women were not in hearing range.

Tom, Sr. smiled at the other men and proclaimed, "Even if I have to wear a darned suit, life just can't get any better than this!"

* * *

After dinner that evening Pete told everyone that he was going to the trout pond. He wanted some time away.

Calli was the main attraction among the women in the kitchen.

Pete smiled and said to Clutch, "Come on Son. You're coming with me." Pete threw a rod over his shoulder and Clutch strolled along at his side. When they arrived at the pond Pete pulled something out of his pocket. It was a red cap with holes notched in to fit over Clutch's ears. Pete wore one that was the same color.

Even though the cap felt awkward to Clutch he wore it with pride. He was quite happy just to be there with his Pete-human. Although Clutch didn't understand everything, he knew they were together. He was quite proud of the two small fish he pulled from the pond and was astonished at the size of the fish Pete caught himself. Both of them were even bigger than Clutch. He didn't even care that Pete's fish were bigger than his. He was spending time with the human he admired the most.

Pete caught another smaller trout and was about to throw it back when he saw the Great Tom Cat of the Woods. Pete called, "Hey Old Buddy!"

The Great Tom Cat looked at him and smiled.

"Come on over here. I've got something for you."

As the older male bobcat walked up to Pete he laid out the fish for him.

The cat rubbed his head against the human's hand before picking up the fish. As he grabbed the tasty, fresh caught trout, he winked at Clutch, who only smiled back.

As Clutch's father headed back to the woods with his fish, Pete and Clutch headed back to the house. When Pete carried the two large trout back to the kitchen to clean them his guests complimented him heavily.

Pete smiled. "I caught a third one, but I shared."

* * *

Friday morning, after the milking and breakfast, Aunt Mae said to Bill, "You'll have to fend for yourself at lunch, and I don't know if I'll be back for dinner either. We ladies are going into Lafayette to get our hair done and enjoy a day of shopping."

Bill said, "That's okay Dear. We guys are going to get our haircuts and enjoy some guy time. Even old Tom is going with us. On top of that, I've hired out the milking and farm work until Monday. I'm taking a couple of days off for family time."

Pete suggested, "Why don't we call over to the Kingman house and we'll all get together at the Country Buffet for dinner at around 7 o'clock?"

Brenda quickly called her grandfather's house to see if these arrangements would be fine with everyone.

Pete did the same with the guests of his house. He would also inform Rob and Broadus.

Brenda would call LeyAnn and Millie.

After Pete made the call to his house he called the restaurant. They assured him that they had a room big enough for his party. He told them, "This will all be on one check. I'll cover it."

All the men headed into town in three cars, leaving ample vehicles for the women to do the same. By 1 o'clock in the afternoon Rob and Broadus met Pete and the other men at the bowling alley for a private tournament among friends. His father-in-law suggested they should spice up the game with a gentleman's wager of a dollar.

By 5:45 the men surrounded the pool tables at the bowling alley.

Later Tom asked his father with a somber expression, "How well did you do Dad?"

The older Tom Kingman smiled. "Let's just say I have a lot more than I came with and leave it at that."

* * *

As everyone in their party was ushered into a small dining room, it was decided that the oldest of the Kingman clan should be called upon to ask the blessing, even though the Reverend James Jenson and his wife had joined the party.

As the aged man closed his eyes and bowed his head he said, "Forgive me for not talking to you for a while. I want to thank you for bringing my family back together. I also want to thank you for giving me a new outlook on things. And most of all, the blessing of the wedding of Pete and Brenda." As he raised his head he said to everyone, "All right. Let's eat, darn it."

They all laughed and headed for the food.

As Pete was putting food onto his plate a man in uniform approached him and asked, "Excuse me Sir. Is your name Pete Dobsin?"

Pete answered with a smile, "Yes it is."

The soldier looked vaguely familiar to him, but he couldn't place him.

"I'm Robert Fisher. We were in basic together."

Pete, realizing who the man was, invited him and his wife to join the party.

The couple graciously accepted.

Pete informed him and his wife that he was getting married tomorrow in Indianapolis. He insisted that, if they didn't have any prior plans, they join them for the wedding.

The couple accepted.

Everyone enjoyed the party and there was much talk considering the events for the following day.

* * *

The next day Uncle Bill decided to sleep late. He had set his alarm for 5 a.m. When he glanced out the window towards the barn he could see, as he already knew, that the milking was already in progress and his animals were being well cared for.

There was a light tapping on his kitchen door. He laughed to himself when he opened it up, already knowing that it would be Pete. "Come on in Son. The coffee's goin'. What's the matter? Wedding jitters?"

"No," said Pete smiling. "I slept like a rock. I'm fully charged and ready to go."

"I'll be the judge of that," interrupted Aunt Mae from the steps. "Sit down boys while I get breakfast cooking." As Aunt Mae served up sausage cakes, flapjacks, and bowls of oatmeal she watched Pete carefully to make sure he wasn't putting pepper in his coffee or ketchup in his oatmeal again. She was satisfied that everything was fine.

Pete said, "Brenda and Calli spent the night at her grandfather's house so I turned in early. I got up around 4:30 like I always do. I've already checked the cows for feed, hay, and water."

Aunt Mae smiled. "Are you ready for today?"

Pete grinned, "I've been ready for this for years. It just took me a while to figure it out. Yes, I'm as ready as I could ever be!"

Uncle Bill said, "We're gonna go into town a little early. We've got something to do in Indy. We're going to pick up Mr. Messinger on the way in. He's closing his store for the whole day." He laughed. "He's real excited. He said he sets people up with perfect rings all the time, but he can now share the joy with them."

Pete smiled and said, "He's been a friend of the family for years. It would be cruel not to invite him."

Everybody agreed.

"So what have you got going this morning Pete?" asked Uncle Bill.

Pete answered, "Brenda and I are going for a walk. We're gonna walk out to the cabin, but she can't see the inside until tonight."

Uncle Bill added, "It'd be smart of you to take extra oil lamps out."

Pete replied, "Dad told me that's the spot where the first cabin was built when our family homesteaded here."

Uncle Bill confirmed, "Yup. They built their cabin by a spring. That well is only twenty-five feet deep, but it has never gone dry."

Pete smiled again. "I can't think of a better place for us to spend our wedding night."

* * *

As Pete and Brenda were walking through the woods later that morning, following the path leading back to the cabin, neither one was paying attention to anything but each other.

Suddenly a bobcat let out a scream and attacked something only fifteen feet in front of them.

Brenda and Pete stood frozen in their steps.

Within seconds the bobcat had killed a very large copperhead snake. When the bobcat was sure the snake was dead he dropped it and walked over to sit directly in front of Pete.

Pete bent over and scratched his ears. "You remember Mr. Whiskers don't you? After all, you named him."

Brenda was a little hesitant at first. He had returned to the wild, but she trusted Pete. She knelt down to scratch Mr. Whiskers' ears.

The older bobcat stretched himself up to where he could rub himself against her cheek purring, then returned to his kill and disappeared into the woods with it.

It was planned that Pete and Brenda would not attend the safety meeting. They would quietly slip into the dressing areas while her father supplied the distraction. It was very common for Wendover Trucking to invite their customers to their social functions, so no one would question who any of the guests were.

At 11:30 am Rob Wendover stepped over to the platform. All of the drivers but four were in attendance. "First of all, I want to thank each and every one of you for your excellent work endeavors. You all are what make this company thrive, and I'm proud of all of you. I'm going to ask all of you to stay throughout the course of the day because we have a lot planned. We've got games for kids of all ages. At about 1 o'clock we'll want everyone in their seats so we can all say goodbye to our friend Too Long. After that we have a surprise for everyone while the charcoal is being prepared to cook the steaks on. This all will take place in the brand new trailer barn. You guys are the best drivers any company could want." He smiled, "To make this an official meeting, remember to wear your seat belts and please remember to use your load bars. I don't want to have to buy another fifty cases of T-bones. By the way folks, we have a lot of our friends visiting us from other states. Try to say hello. Go have fun! That's an order!"

* * *

At 1 o'clock everyone made their way into the trailer barn where there were many rows of chairs up in front. Jimmy Jenson and his lovely wife walked up to the microphone. "I have been selected to speak to you because I'm used to standing in front of a congregation. First off, I want to thank all of you for coming today. It is indeed a beautiful day. I would also like to thank our honored guests from out of town, our customers, who have taken their valuable time, and the drivers and their families, as well as their support staff. We have here today a man who has been with Wendover Trucking for so long that he was with Wendover before it existed as a company. He finally got smart enough to retire. Our own Thomas Kingman, after all these years, has wised up enough to go home and stay there. To honor this man, some of us will come up here to share memories of him."

Several people took their turns speaking of their memories of Tom Kingman. All the while, no one knew of the events that were taking shape.

Jim looked over the group as a shepherd watching over his flock. He smiled as his wife gave a slight nod of her head.

When Vonell finished speaking her kind words of Tom Kingman, Tom himself was called to the microphone. Tom merely stood before the group and said to them, "I can not begin to tell you what this day means to me. It's only right that today's events be shared with all of you. I can honestly say that this is the most joyous event we could ever hope for. We have all waited too long. Thank you."

With that the band members took their places on the stage.

Once again Jim took his place at the microphone. Jim looked out at the group and then requested, "I would like all of you to stand while I ask for a blessing for this man and his wife, then for the events of this day. Afterward, I will turn this over to the band. I will ask you to stand a bit longer to greet the person beside you." As Jim launched into his prayer, everyone closed their eyes and lowered their heads. At that point LeyAnn, Millie, Broadus, and Rob all took their places.

As the prayer ended everyone was astonished when the band began to play the 'Wedding March.' When everyone started looking around they noticed, to their surprise, Pete and Brenda proceeding down the aisle with Clutch and Calli faithfully by their sides.

Red Dog hollered out, "Now this is what I call a party!"

Everyone else fell silent when the couple stood in front of their minister and friend to be joined together in matrimony. When the minister called for the rings Pete released the beautiful wedding band for Brenda. She untied Pete's gold wedding band from Calli's pretty flowered hat. As the two exchanged their vows and placed the rings on each other's fingers, everyone cheered and applauded.

Finally Rob took the microphone and called the crowd to silence. "We hope everyone enjoyed the wedding, and now, I'm told, the BBQ pits are ready to cook. We will set up a bucket if anyone wishes to leave a tip for this wonderful couple. Go have fun!"

Crystal and Edwin had set up their cameras, catching the entire event on film. Amongst all the festivities Rob Wendover again called for the attention of everyone. He then introduced Crystal and Edwin. He said, "All of you drivers know these two as some of the best paying customers at Wendover. They have an announcement that they wish to make. I ask that you give them your full attention."

Crystal took the microphone and said, "All of you are aware of our import-export business and our biggest seller, our calendars. With great pride my husband and I would like to announce the first place winners of our online contest and award the prize of $10,000 and a year's supply of products out of our catalog to Clutch and Calli, owned by Pete and Brenda Dobsin. This time, let's have a round of applause for what will be the two most famous kittens in the world this year." Then, looking at Clutch and Calli, "And the two best dressed."

Once again everyone cheered loudly.

Pete and Brenda were then asked to say a few words.

Pete spoke briefly. "This is the most wonderful day of my life. I wish I could express what each and every one of you here means to us. We are both honored that you could share this day with us."

Brenda's grandfather hollered loudly over the applause, "Kiss her again Son! I won't whip your butt this time!"

Tom Kingman, Jr. extended his hand for the microphone. "I want to thank everyone for the careful planning of this wedding; the dispatchers who made sure the drivers were in, all of our out of town guests for taking time out of their busy schedules to honor my little girl and best friend, and, most of all, Rob and Millie Wendover for making all of our dreams come true for this day—even if I did have to wear a suit. Pete, I hope you and Brenda are both as happy as

Phyllis and I are. Rob, I still want to turn you over my knee! Thank you very much."

Uncle Bill and Aunt Mae took the kittens home with them while Pete and Brenda slipped away for some privacy.

* * *

Sunday morning the sanctuary of the small county chapel was overflowing.

When the service ended, the minister addressed the congregation. "I wish to formally introduce Mr. and Mrs. Peter Dobsin, Jr. I also wish to offer praise to their families, who have been no stranger to tragedies." He then announced that a reception would be held at the Dobsin home at 1 o'clock that afternoon. All were invited.

* * *

That afternoon, while the humans all gathered at Pete and Brenda's home for their party, Clutch and Calli gathered with the other animals in the meadow.

Clutch and Calli told the story to the other animals. They told the other animals about being part of the wonderful wedding the previous day, then added that they would all be leaving in a few days to start a new adventure as a family.

Calli informed the council of animals that, while their humans committed to each other the day before, she and Clutch had done the same.

There was a great joyous noise from all the animals.

When the crowd of animals settled down Miss Della approached Clutch and said, "How about it Clutch, there's a position that could open in security. It's yours if you want it."

Clutch smiled and boldly answered, "Thank you Aunt Della, but I can't. I'm a trucking cat—Clutch the Trucking Cat."